TIMBER PIRATES

BORGO PRESS BOOKS BY ARDATH MAYHAR

The Absolutely Perfect Horse (with Marylois Dunn)
Carrots and Miggle
Crazy Quilt: The Best Short Stories of Ardath Mayhar
Deadly Memoir: A Novel of Suspense
The Door in the Hill: A Tale of the Turnipins
The Dropouts: A Tale of Growing Up in East Texas
Feud at Sweetwater Creek: A Novel of the Old West
The Fugitives: A Tale of Prehistoric Times
The Heirs of Three Oaks: A Novel of the Old West
How the Gods Wove in Kyrannon: Tales of the Triple Moons
Hunters of the Plains: A Novel of Prehistoric America
Island in the Lake: A Novel of Native America
Khi to Freedom: A Science Fiction Novel
The Lintons of Skillet Bend
Lone Runner: A Novel of the Old West
Lords of the Triple Moons: Tales of the Triple Moons
Makra Choria: A Novel of High Fantasy
Medicine Dream: The Further Adventures of Burr Henderson
Messengers in White: A Science Fantasy Novel
Monkey Station (Macaque Cycle #1; with Ron Fortier)
People of the Mesa: A Novel of Native America
A Planet Called Heaven: A Science Fiction Novel
Prescription for Danger: A Novel of the Old West
Reflections; &, Journey to an Ending: Collected Poems
A Road of Stars: A Fantasy of Life, Death, Love, and Art
Runes of the Lyre: A Science Fantasy Novel
The Saga of Grittel Sundotha: A Science Fantasy Novel
The Seekers of Shar-Nuhn: Tales of the Triple Moons
*Slewfoot Sally and the Flying Mule: Tall Tales from Cotton
    County, Texas*
Soul-Singer of Tyrnos: A Fantasy Novel
Strange Doings in the Pine Hills: Stories of Fantasy and Mystery
Through a Stone Wall: Lessons from Thirty Years of Writing
Timber Pirates: A Novel of East Texas (with Marylois Dunn)
Towers of the Earth: A Novel of Native America
Trail of the Seahawks (Macaque Cycle #2; with Ron Fortier)
Warlock's Gift: Tales of the Triple Moons
The World Ends in Hickory Hollow
A World of Weirdities: Tales to Shiver By

TIMBER PIRATES

A Novel of East Texas

by

Marylois Dunn

and

Ardath Mayhar

The Borgo Press
An Imprint of Wildside Press LLC

MMVIII

CONTENTS

FOREWORD

Marylois Dunn and I have been friends for more that sixty years. Sharing our love for books through our youth, we both became published authors by the time we were middle-aged, and *Timber Pirates* was the second novel on which we collaborated. Marylois originated the plot while she was a librarian in Houston, but later she encouraged me to add my own touches, for we each had long experience in and of the East Texas woods country. We think it came out quite well.

—Ardath Mayhar
Chireno, Texas
September 2006

CHAPTER ONE

Spring though it was, the sun was already hot. On the shadeless school grounds it had reached almost summer intensity. Beau was only vaguely aware of that, though. He was hot with a fiercer, inner heat. He knew that his face was flushed, and his teeth were gritted so hard that he could hardly get the words out.

"You call my brother a thief—I call you a liar! A dirty Redbone liar!"

Redbone was the worst insult any woods-boy could lay a tongue to. Beau crouched, waiting and facing his tormentor. His bony body was hunched for the fight that he knew must happen, this time. He shoved back a curling lock of flame-red hair with one wrist, but his blue eyes never left the big shape of Gaitor Morfew.

Beau saw Gaitor grin. "Andy's a thief, all right. Why else would the sheriff take him to ask him questions?" His grin wasn't as easy as he would have liked.

Beau knew to be called a Redbone was something he couldn't take. Not that the Redbones were bad—they mostly lived way back in the Sabine River bayous and bothered no one, but the thought of the mixed heritage of red and black and white was something the ignorant woods-people, like Gaitor didn't want applied to themselves.

Gaitor flexed his big arms. Two years older than thirteen-year-old Beau, he outweighed him by thirty pounds. He had pushed Beau for this fight for a week. Now, at last, Beau was going to give him what he wanted, the chance to beat the smaller boy with much enjoyment. Gaitor was always muttering that those Hartleys had no business holding their fiery-red heads so high, keeping themselves to themselves as if they were better than other folks.

Beau dug his moccasins more firmly into the white sand and waited, still in a crouch. He knew that he wouldn't be able to whip Gaitor, nobody ever had, but he reckoned to give him a good round for his money. No matter what happened, Gaitor would know he'd been in a fight. Nobody was going to call Andy a thief and get away with it.

As if tired of waiting, the bigger boy leaned forward and cuffed Beau on the side of his head. Beau's wits whirled for an instant, but he didn't wait for them to settle down. He stepped in, arms working like pistons, and pounded Gaitor's well-padded ribs. To reach for the taller boy's face would lay him open to too much punishment, he knew, so he concentrated on the midriff, as Andy had taught him.

"If you aim to fight," Andy had said, "go for the closest spot that you can hit straight from the shoulder. Too high or too low, and you lose the force of your blow."

He got in about six good hard licks, hearing Gaitor grunt at each one. He took several he didn't bother to count. Mrs. Terry was upon him before he heard her coming, and Mr. Andrews, the Ag.-P.E. teacher, was pulling on Gaitor.

"Stop it! You boys quit that this minute! You know better than this, both of you!" Mr. Andrews sounded angry.

Beau stepped back, ashamed. The P.E. teacher had no use for troublemakers. He made it known that by the seventh grade, boys ought to be civilized enough not to fight, even if they were woods-people. Beau liked and respected the man, and he felt that he was right, most of the time.

Andrews was a bit gruff, to cover his innate good nature, and he padded out his meager salary by working hard on his small farm, which adjoined the Hartley's big holding. He refused to let the boys call him "coach." He said that in a school too small to field any kind of a team, that would be pretentious. He was a good man, and Beau was sorry for making him angry.

"Beau! You promised me. No more fighting!" Mrs. Terry became red-faced when she was upset, and she was very excitable. She got upset over a lot of things that seemed trivial to him. Still, he knew quite well that fighting on school grounds was a serious offense. The only worse things were being caught with drugs in your possession or having a knife on your person.

Gaitor didn't look ashamed at all. He stood solidly on his big feet, looking mean and defiant. He should have known he was in worse trouble than Beau; fighting a younger, smaller boy was considered unforgivable. Whatever the Principal did, Gaitor seemed to think that his Pa would forgive him, as he'd gotten in trouble over a Hartley. Pa would back him, any time, against a Hartley.

Beau, winded and panting, swiped at the cut over his eye that was oozing a thin stream of blood. He looked up at Mrs. Terry, who was, after all, his teacher and almost a friend in spite of that.

"I've stood all his bad-mouthing my brother that I can take," he wheezed. "I didn't mean to break my promise. I really am sorry, but I can't take no more than what I can take!" He was still too angry to pick his words for grammar, as Mrs. Terry kept urging him to do.

Mr. Andrews put a firm hand on the shoulder of each boy and propelled them before him across the playground, into the white stone building. Mrs. Terry, left to watch the playground, caught Beau's eye as he moved away. She looked hurt. But she scattered the knot of onlookers back into their groups and their games. He could hear the yelling start up again, before he reached the building.

This was not the first time Beau had made the short trek down the hall to the Principal's office. Gaitor had made the trip even oftener than he had, he knew. This was the first time they had ever gone there together, and Beau was uncomfortable facing his reckoning with his enemy right beside him.

Beau sat stiffly, edging onto one of the worn ladderback chairs. He would have liked to lean back nonchalantly, as Gaitor was doing, with one arm flung over the back of the chair. He was not as defiant as the older boy and he wasn't tall enough to do it without looking ridiculous.

He knew that Gaitor Morfew's Pa didn't worry about his son's constant trips to the office. Old Morfew obeyed very few rules in his own life, and he didn't really expect Gaitor and his older brother, Taintor, to either. Beau had often wondered why Mr. Morfew bothered to force Gaitor to go to school at all. Down here in the boondocks nobody paid much attention, once a boy reached twelve or so. The big, hard-headed boy hated being in school instead of out in the woods.

Andy was another story. He took his job as father-figure of the Hartley young ones seriously. He had a lot to worry about. He managed the timber resources that were the family's only source of income. He had promised, long ago, a lick at home for every one received at school. He lived up to that word. If Beau was badly in the wrong, Andy's licks outdid those the teachers gave by a big margin.

Thinking about what would come at home, Beau almost missed the end of the lecture and Mr. Rogers' question. He caught it just in time.

"Yessir. I guess I'm ready for my licks," he gulped and bent over.

Mr. Andrews paused long enough to make sure there was nothing in any of his pockets that would soften or unduly stiffen the impact of the paddle. Waiting for his collection of rocks to be disposed of, Beau caught Gaitor's delighted grin. A grin that made him so angry that it was no trouble to take his three licks without flinching.

Gaitor bent over, his square face glum. He got three for fighting, three more for picking on a smaller and younger boy. Beau thought that Mr. Andrews put more enthusiasm into the licks he gave Gaitor. When the big boy straightened, he snarled, "I'm gonna tell Pa you made a difference. You didn't give that Hartley but half as many licks. He ain't a-gonna like it!"

Mr. Rogers' face flushed bright red. He was a quiet little man, neat and precise in his ways. With the limited facilities and the more limited supply of money at his disposal, he managed to run a good school.

He didn't understand the woods people, even after fifteen years, but he always tried to be scrupulously fair. This accusation was both unjust and untrue.

"You go ahead and tell him, Gaitor. And while you're telling, say that you've just gotten yourself expelled from school. Again. If he doesn't come in to talk to me about your behavior, it's going to be for good, this time."

Gaitor looked stunned. "I took my licking. You can't put me out!"

"Oh yes, I can," Mr. Rogers said, "I just did. You've made trouble for your schoolmates, your teachers, Mr. Andrews, and me all the way through since the first grade. Now you're big enough to do a lot of damage, and you've begun picking on the younger ones. I've taken all your sass that I intend to. You are out!"

Gaitor hadn't bargained for this. Beau knew if his Pa was sober enough to understand the word Gaitor took to him, he wasn't going to like it. When he really sobered up, wow! Knowing that he'd have to stay sober long enough to make the trip in to see Rogers would make him even angrier. Beau was glad he was not in Gaitor's shoes.

When the older boy passed him, with a mean sideways grimace, Beau knew that he hadn't heard the end of this incident. He rose to follow Gaitor out, but Mr. Andrews caught his arm.

"Just a minute, Beaumont."

Beau shuddered. He hated that name ever since he got old enough to know what it was.

"I wish you'd tell us what it was that Gaylord said about your brother to make you so angry."

Beau considered. He hated to dirty his mouth with repeating the lie. Still, Rogers and Andrews had always been fair to him, and he respected them both. He sighed.

"I guess you've heard what everyone else is saying. Gaitor just pushed it too far. When the sheriff takes someone in and charges them with stealing, it don't make a difference to most folks that he can't make it stick. Just the fact that the sheriff asked Andy a lot of questions makes a lot of the people 'round here think it's Andy that's been taking timber in the National Forest. Gaitor's been needling me for a week, ever since it happened, as if he wanted to make me fight him, now I think it over."

"But why did Sheriff Ralls take Andy in, anyway? He ought to know better than to think he'd steal."

"Andy thought he knew better; he didn't seem to."

"Ralls is new to this part of the state, isn't he?" Mr. Rogers asked. He wasn't looking at Beau, this time, so the boy said nothing.

Andrews nodded. "He's been here about a year longer than you have. He came in just before you transferred here from Covington, over near the Angelina. Ralls came in to fill in, after Ben Oates died, and he was pretty good at the job, so he got himself elected to office, when the special election came up." Mr. Andrews looked sharply at Beau.

"Exactly what did he charge Andy with, Beau?"

"Didn't charge him at all," Beau answered. "Took him in and questioned him almost all night. He'd had a 'nonymous letter that said Andy was one of the 'timber pirates' who's been creaming the pole pine off the National Forest land."

"Do you suppose he just thought that Andy knew something about it? outside of what is common knowledge and without being mixed up in the thievery?"

Beau looked up at the two men and thought for a long moment before answering. "He knows what everyone else knows. Just that somebody is slipping in to the good stands of pine in spots that don't get much watching over. Stealing the richest trees. Nothing more than that."

He didn't want to discuss the thing any more. He felt sick to think that anyone, even an outlander like Ralls, could think that Andy would have anything to do with such goings-on. He was relieved when the two men seemed to understand his reluctance to say anything more.

They returned him to class with a firm reminder that there was to be no more fighting, no matter what.

The fifth period had already begun when he slipped into his seat. The afternoon went by in a kind of haze, and he half-listened without really hearing. Only the fact that he liked history and had read the lesson allowed him to answer Mrs. Witcher's questions automatically. When he got into Mrs. Terry's room for the last period, he was relieved to find that she didn't expect too much out of him. She let him sit quietly, reading his lesson, and he was grateful for that.

When the bell rang, he didn't join the orderly rush out of the door to freedom. Instead, he stood beside Mrs. Terry's desk until she looked up.

"What is it, Beau?"

"I wanted to tell you that I'm sorry about the fight at lunch. I got so mad I forgot my promise."

She looked at him steadily for a moment. Then she leaned her elbows on the desk and smiled faintly.

"Well, Beau, I've taught Gaitor—Gaylord—" She corrected herself quickly, "As well as you, and he isn't an easy person to get along with, sometimes. Still, fighting doesn't settle anything. You just get into trouble, and Gaylord will still say anything in the world he pleases."

"He'd better not!" Beau clenched his fists and felt his face grow red again.

"But he will, Beau. He's that kind of person, I'm sorry to say. Some people seem to get their pleasure from being hateful and downgrading others. Do you know why?"

He shook his head.

"Because, deep inside, they secretly believe that the person they gossip about is a more exciting person, maybe a better person, than they are. By saying ugly things about him, the gossiper tries to hurt or destroy him. Someone who always bad-mouths others is really to be pitied."

"It's hard for me to feel sorry for Gait...uh, Gaylord," the boy said.

Mrs. Terry smiled again. "I know. I don't really expect you to. But you do understand what I'm trying to say, don't you?"

"That I shouldn't fight Gaylord, because he knows he's not as good as me so why give him a chance to whip me?" Beau said it in one breath, and more as a statement than as a question.

She laughed heartily until she had to wipe her eyes. "That is not what I said at all. Still, I guess the idea is the same, generally. Beaumont, you've done so well at controlling that terrible temper of yours. Don't let it get the upper hand again. It's like being a slave, with your own temper the master. You've got to stay on top of it. Promise me."

Beau promised that he wouldn't lose his temper. He was careful not to renew his promise not to fight. He'd hold off on that one for awhile.

Once he was out in the schoolyard again, his eleven-year-old brother Arthur joined him. "Andy's going to swat you for sure, Beau. What'd you go fighting for?"

"I've talked about it more, already, than I want to. Come on, we'll miss the bus."

Arthur wasn't ever easy to put off. "Who was winning?" he panted, hurrying along at his side toward the rank of waiting yellow school buses.

"Neither one yet. hadn't had time. We was just getting started good."

They trotted up just as their own bus opened its doors to let on the jostling crowd of youngsters. Beau managed to separate himself from Arthur in the press of getting on. He didn't try for his usual back seat but contented himself with one near the front. The Humacre twins, Shelly and Sharon, squeezed onto the worn plastic seat with him, but he didn't mind too much. The little girls played with his small sister Violet while their father fished the Big Sandy Creek, which wasn't too far from Beau's home. He knew they'd spend the entire trip talking to each other and wouldn't bother him with questions, so he was pleased with the arrangement.

He opened his history book and pretended great interest in Napoleon's long-ago problems. Apparently he put on a good act, because nobody bothered him all the way home, though the usual shouting and teasing and quarrelling went on all around him. The only time he glanced up was when Solly Masters hung little Bob Tucker halfway out of the window until the driver stopped the bus, threatened to whip all the bigger boys who put him up to it and to throw him off the bus for good. Then things quieted down a bit.

Over the edge of his book, Beau stared out the window ahead and to one side of him. The afternoon sun was slanting down through the trees, casting blue shadows onto the pale dust of the road. The ride was familiar, yet Beau was seeing the tree-arched road, the circling forest more sharply than ever before.

He wanted desperately to cry. Of course, he was too old to cry, and he wasn't by himself, so it was out of the question. Yet all the terrible problems of the past weeks seemed to fall on him at once.

On Christmas Day everything began. That had always been a very special day for the Hartleys. Being wood folks, they observed the old customs that came down to them from the very first Hartley to settle in East Texas. Christmas meant getting down the family Bible for the reading of the Christmas story, and that was something special, right there.

19

That ragged leather volume was their file, their record-book, and their family history, all in one. Whichever one of the family was to do the reading turned the yellowed pages very carefully.

They had a good Christmas. After their meal of roast venison haunch, they opened the gifts. Then everyone sat around the big fireplace for the reading. In the middle of it, Maggie, their very old hound, raised her head and growled softly in her throat. Her "Somebody's coming" growl. Only then did the others hear the sound of a car on the dirt road.

Andy went to the door and waited, peering out into the gray day. "It's Chris," he said, over his shoulder.

He came back, bringing with him Chris Garrison, the assistant ranger for the National Forest. Chris's young face showed embarrassment as he spoke. "I'm sorry to come barging in on your Christmas, but we've just discovered that about fifty acres of pole pine has been cut on some of the National Forest land that backs onto your line. I'd like Andy to come with me, if he will. Maybe he can figure out how they took it out and where they might have taken it."

Ma hadn't liked it a bit. Christmas was a day for family. She knew it was an emergency, and she agreed that Andy should go, particularly since the theft took place so near their own property line. Thieves wouldn't make any difference between stealing government timber and stealing Hartley timber. Ma delayed them for long enough to size up the young ranger. Only Andy had met Chris, until now. He went to the chief ranger, Mr. Walker, for help in marking out some timber he wanted to cut for sale, and Chris was sent to cruise the timber with him.

Beau understood why Ma had insisted that the young ranger must come back with Andy for supper. He was a good person—you could see that in his honest brown eyes, even in the careless lock of dark hair that he kept pushing out of his eyes without realizing he was doing it.

Supper had been something more than suppers after Christmas dinner usually managed to be. At that time Beau had been too absorbed in what the two men found in the woods to pay full attention to what he was eating.

A small crew, both agreed. Five or six men at most to do the cutting. They carefully cut only prime trees, aiming them so that their falls were hidden from an overhead view to avoid detection by helicopter patrols. A careful faller could lay his tree in such a way that it didn't crush smaller trees or break branches from larger ones as it went down. By cutting only a few prime trees out of one stand, the thieves made certain that the dark umbrella of pine tops still spread thickly enough to mask the missing trees.

"I don't know why they'd go to so much trouble, going way back in there," Andy seemed puzzled. "It's almost as if they weren't really after the stuff they took, but that's all there is back there. Timber."

"They had two big trucks, one light truck, probably and A-frame to load with, and a jeep, a lot of equipment to take in for so few trees. There's a funny feeling about this, all right." Chris said.

"There are better stands of pine much nearer the main roads. Handier, and not so risky. This way, they crossed onto your land a couple of times as they snaked in and out. We've been cruising up that way. We haven't seen or heard anything like saws or trucks, and those sounds would bring us up short, so far from any road. I don't see how we could have missed hearing such activity."

"They might be working weekends, or at night. Dangerous business, felling trees at night, but that must be it. Nobody is within ten miles of that stand, at those times." Andy's face was tense, beneath his berry-bush crown of red hair.

At that time, Beau remembered, Chris hadn't seemed to suspect Andy of having anything at all to do with the piracy. Later, when the sheriff hauled Andy in for questioning, Chris went with him and defended him hotly. The thefts had not stopped— they continued and became worse than ever. The sheriff seemed frantic to make an arrest, right or wrong.

Only when Chris went and got Farris Palmer, the local banker, to come into the courthouse and assure the sheriff that Andy, while not rich, was certainly not badly in need of money did the sheriff give up on charging him in the crime.

The sheriff was hot about it. He claimed that the tire-tracks of some of the pirates' trucks and those of Andy's trucks were identical. "To make it airtight, somebody saw the timber-thieves driving away from one of their cuts," he insisted. "He said one of the drivers had hair the same color as Andy's."

With only circumstantial evidence, he couldn't

charge Andy formally just on account of the color of his hair. He did warn him that he'd be watched very carefully. He was, too, but the thefts went on, un-hindered and uncaught. The sheriff still thought Andy was in on the series of thefts, and others, hun-gry for something of interest to chew on, took up the tale.

The bus gave a lurch, heaving onto the wooden bridge leading to the sand road. Beau woke from his musing and knew that, two miles further on, he and Arthur would climb down and walk the last mile and a half to the house. He put his books together, handy for carrying. Then he thought of something. They could get off right here and walk over to the spot in the woods where Andy was working this week.

He stood up, balancing against the sway of the bus. Arthur, seeing him, began getting ready to get off, too.

"Mr. Thrash!" he called, "Please let us off here." The driver slowed the bus to a halt. He knew that the boys were on their own land and would get home without trouble.

"Andy working close by?" he asked, working the lever that opened the flip-flap door. There was something not quite right about his voice, but Beau forced himself not to notice it.

"All this week. He's sold some hickory for rail-road ties. Getting it out of the creek bottom over yonder." He gestured vaguely in the wrong direc-tion. Somehow, he didn't feel like giving anything to anybody, right now.

He followed Arthur out into the chilly march evening. Though it was still early, the masses of trees cut off the sunlight from the road, and he shivered. A long time seemed to have passed since he stood in the hot sand of the schoolyard and fought with Gaitor. Losing himself in the past hadn't helped him to find any clue to the steadily mounting pile of troubles that seemed to loom over the Hartleys.

Chapter Two

Gaitor Morfew didn't ride his usual bus. His brother, Taintor, was in town with the beat-up old pickup, he knew, and he walked the few blocks to the hitch yard, where Taintor would be shooting the breeze with whoever happened to be there. There were always the farmers, with their loads of produce for sale to the town ladies. Sometimes a trucker would be there with a load of Valley citrus or Arkansas apples, and there would be tall tales of sights and adventures along the way.

Most of the town children walked that way, even if they lived in the opposite direction. They thought a whaling a small price to pay to hear the cussing and the stories and to see the leathery men spit accurate streams of tobacco juice into small cans set at many feet's distance. Those who glanced back and saw Gaitor following them seemed to decide, suddenly, that today was the day they'd get home on time. Soon the big boy was walking alone up the bit of oil-top street leading to the hitch yard. That tickled his vanity, for he prided himself on being the most feared student still in school.

He wasn't still in school! The thought jolted him. Not that he liked school or learned much of anything there, but his Pa, at the tag-end of a life of broken promises, most of them to his wife, was hanging on to that last one he had made her with bulldog tenacity. His boys were going to graduate from school if he had to break all their bones to manage it. Taintor had done that, by the skin of his teeth. Gaitor slid back almost as much as he was promoted, but he was now within four years of that goal. Pa was going to give it to him good, he had no doubt.

He looked ahead. The rusty-dappled blue of the pickup was readily visible, parked in the shade of one of the big sycamores at the side of the parking area. Taintor was hitched halfway sitting on one fender, listening to someone who looked familiar, Cousin Garwood. They were talking business, Gaitor knew, but he couldn't wait on that.

"Hey, Tain!" he called, breaking into a trot across the mangy grass beside the oil top, "let's head for home. I got throwed out of school, this noon, and we got to tell the old man."

Taintor had been a hard-nosed older brother, always. He'd never given Gaitor an inch of elbow-room, and the younger boy had gotten almost more beatings from his brother than from his father. Still, Taintor had the primal family feeling that seemed born in the woods people. When danger threatened, he rallied around his own.

With a brusque nod to Cousin Garwood, the big man climbed into the truck and hit the starter, which ground noisily. Gaitor was in his seat and shutting the door by the time it caught up into a ragged roar.

"Gotta tune this thing up," Taintor grumbled. "Runs like a jackhammer. Now what's all this about school?"

As they bounced and rumbled and stuttered down the rutted tracks that led back into the sand-hills that were the Morfew holding, Gaitor told his story. His brother said nothing, though he grunted from time to time. His eyes were on the uneven road, and his expression never changed.

After Gaitor was done, he drove for a long time without saying anything. Then he spoke.

"Rogers said if Pa'd come in and see him, he'd let you come back?"

"Said maybe he'd let me come back. You know Pa ain't gonna like having to gussy up and go into Town. You know he ain't."

Taintor swung around a sharp bend that barely missed a gigantic sweet gum tree, gunned the engine to send the truck up a steep slope, and killed the motor in the shadow of the chinaberry that shaded half their sandy yard. Then he turned and eyed Gaitor.

"Ain't gonna like it, but he'll do it. You know it and I know it, but you're gonna have sore bones for a week, young'un. Come on. Let's hope he's mellow-drunk and not bitter-drunk."

Before they reached the gap-planked porch, they could hear Pa talking. They stopped in their tracks. All his different drunken moods were familiar. They knew exactly how to handle all of them, except for this one in which he talked and talked to their dead mother. At this time he was unpredictable as a tornado, and just about as dangerous.

"Let's wait out here for a while," Taintor whispered. Gaitor nodded gratefully. The two sat quietly on the edge of the porch, swinging their feet. Parson, their flea-bitten hound, came out from under the porch, smelled their feet, and thumped his al-most hairless tail in the powdery sand below them. He looked worried, as well he might. He knew Turbo Morfew at least as well as the man's sons did, and he had to stay with him most of the time.

Morfew's voice was clear and loud. One of his peculiarities was that he never slurred his words when he was drunk and he never staggered. They could hear his footsteps, as he walked his proverbial straight line, back and forth across the pine-plank floor of the main room. Talking. Talking.

"You see, Sadie," he was saying, "it wasn't that I didn't care fer you. I just never was none fer making over a person. Losing my land, that mighty near killed me, and you know it.

"If it hadn't been fer that gover'ment fellow, what was his name? It's gone now, but he was the onliest thing that kept me from taking my gun in hand and dying right on that ground they took away from me. He was a good man. Growed up in the woods, for all his college and working for the gover'ment. He was the one showed me that this sandy tag-end of the place might be worth something, had something I could use and love like the part they took away did.

"Lord, he taken to the deep woodsy place! I showed him the jack-in-the-pulpits fixing to come out and the May-apples blooming. We talked tim-ber, down there, and he showed me how by cutting out some of the hardwood you could make the pine grow. He'd look up and up at the big hickories and ashes and oak trees in the low land, and I could see in his eyes how it hurt him to think of their being cut to make room for some fool lake. I'd tell him

28

about the tree Grampa climbed to get away from the bear, and the hickory that we kids used to go to get nuts for Ma's Christmas hickory-nut cake, and I could see he knowed how much I loved that land.

"He knowed it was my land, and so did the gover'ment. Nobody never said it wasn't. The papers said so, all in Spanish, deeded proper to my great grampappy. Right on down to Grampa and Pa and me. Ten sections of land, over six thousand acres, that was give to my family, so much for every child and growed-up in the family.

"Jem Cutcheon tried to help me out, if he did work for the gover'ment. He told 'em that my folks had put their blood into that land. They fought Mex'kins, and they fought land-grabbers, and then they fought off carpetbaggers.

"But no. Got to have water down to Beaumont, they told us. Got to have recreation for the city folks. Nobody give a thought to the sweet little creeks running down to the big river that would be gone forever. Nobody cared about the wild pink azaleas and the big dogwoods that made it like— like fairyland in the springtime. Or the little sundews catching insects in their red-fringed mouths. Didn't nobody care about the critters that had denned and hunted and birthed and died in those woods since time began. They was all mine to care for; my land, my critters, my plants.

"In spite of everything, they taken it away from me. Oh, they give me money to take its place, but money ain't land. Money didn't help the old cinnamon-bear sow when the water come into her cave in the deep hollow. Money didn't help the bobcats and the panthers, when the lake drove 'em out into the farmlands so the 'sportsmen' from the city could kill 'em and stuff their hides. The wolves moved up-country and give the farmers fits with their live-stock, until they had to be hunted down and shot or trapped. All because the land wasn't mine no more.

"There ain't no fighting the gover'ment, once it makes up its mind to something. One man and his little bit of land don't mean nothing to the big-hats and the white shirts in Washington."

The listening boys heard the thump of one big fist into the other hand. They knew that tears would be streaming down the seamed face, and their father's pale-blue eyes would be red with weeping. Then the voice started again, and the sons sighed and slumped on the porch.

"They let me keep this strip. Two thousand acres, where the lake didn't reach. I moved our house, log by log, did you know that, Sadie? Wasn't going to let the water get the house my folks built, where our boys were born. I even moved the fire-place, and you know that had come down through four different houses on the same spot. We had to leave the deep silent pines for the chattery ruckus of the sand hill hardwoods. Hardwoods is a poor sub-stitute, but what could I do? I never liked this part of the place, but it was still mine. Still a part of the home place that great grampa earned and died on.

"But, Lord, Lord, Sadie, after we moved out, they come with heavy machinery. Bulldozers and saws and trucks. They logged off the big stuff, cut the pines and the hickories, and then they bulldozed all the smaller trees. All the deep, pretty places was all scraped clean, and the land was open and raw and ugly. All the little creeks that had trickled through the woods were bleeding red-dirt runoff like streams of blood. It was enough to drive a woods-loving man clean out of his senses. The little animals, they ran around looking for their lost homes, their lost trails. The poor little deer tried to move across country and got run over by cars and trucks that they never had knowed about before and couldn't stay out of the way of.

"Jem hurt right along with me, but he was just a working man like me. There was nothing he could do to make things right. He said it'd take a hundred years for things to heal up there. For the forest to find its way back around the edges, and the critters to settle down and prosper again. A hundred years. No wonder God don't let men live too long.

"I hate this place, Sadie. I hate the way the hickories talk in the wind. I hate the sandy ground and the woods that lets the sun through. But the woods are gone, the ones I loved. The bears are gone, and the panthers. Only a few bobcats are still toughing it out, and the deer."

The boys on the porch heard a sob, deep racking man-tears for the lost world that had been Turbo Morfew's haven. He never had cried for their mother.

"No use talking to him now," whispered Taintor. "He won't be fit to talk to for a week. You might as well make up your mind to come in and work with me full time, Gaitor. I been needing you, anyways. We're a tad short-handed."

They rose cautiously and left the porch. Pastor, seeing them head for the woods, fell in behind them, wagging his pitiful tail. Anything was better than staying at home and hearing his master cry.

CHAPTER THREE

Beau and Arthur stood for a moment, after the school bus turned itself ponderously in a logging track and headed back for the main road. Early in the afternoon, it was also early in the year. The shadows were long over the pale sand of the road.

"We going over to the cut?" Arthur asked, as his brother seemed to hesitate.

"Might as well go ahead and tell Andy and get the whole thing over with," Beau sighed.

"Beat you there." Arthur shouted over his shoulder, charging ahead to get the lead he knew he must have if he were to beat Beau to the clearing. Beau followed him at a slow trot. Just enough to keep Arthur running, but not fast enough to wind himself. He wasn't all that anxious to see Andy right now.

Brother or not, Andy was the nearest thing to a father that Beau and the younger ones had or even remembered, more than vaguely. Of course, Beau had been old enough to have memories of Pa. Being lifted in oak-like arms, tussling and tickling on the rag rug in front of the fireplace, but he'd never had time to develop the closeness that Andy had felt for Pa. He felt that kind of thing for Andy.

There had been two older brothers than Andy.

Elmer had died in the same accident as Pa, and Ma was as close-mouthed about him as she was about her dead husband. Skipper joined the Navy shortly after the terrible accident. He didn't come back from Vietnam. Funny to think that he'd be a man in his thirties, now.

Only Andy was left of the older children, and Andy was a woods man to the bone. A redhead like Beau, he lacked Beau's fiery temper. He was easy-going, and his quick grin betrayed him, many times, when he was trying to be a stern father to his brood of sisters and brothers. He let Beau follow him through the woods just the way, long ago, he had followed their father. He taught the boy the things he had been taught:

How to live with the forest without fighting it. How to track critters, how to identify every plant that grew, and how to listen to what the trees and the wind and the very silences themselves said.

Beau guessed that he knew Andy better than anyone else in the world. Better even than their mother. He supposed that nobody but he knew how much it hurt Andy to let anyone come into this particular timber-stand for cutting.

This was the last part of the original woods. Dense and virginal, the heavy-branched trees covered with polypodium and Virginia creeper and poison ivy, the huge-boled pines with their ever-sighing umbrellas of needles spread away over almost a whole section of land, more than six hundred acres. The soil underfoot was springy humus. Where wind had toppled a tree to let in sunlight through the dense canopy of leaves and needles, the ground-layer was tightly woven with chokeberry and saw vine and dewberry. Trumpet vine blazed its orange bugles there in summer. Sumac burned brown-red in fall.

The dominant feature was the pine. Tremendous pines four men couldn't reach around with their hands joined, together with the ranks of young seedlings that sprang up everywhere there might be a patch of sunlight to give them encouragement. In and out among the stands of dogwood, redbud, oak, gum, catalpa, walnut and wild cherry danced the infant pine trees. Doomed to wither and die, most of them, through overcrowding or lack of light. The scent of pine dominated the woods.

Pine trees, Andy had told him, dominated the Hartleys, too. Though Andy had only a high school education, he did well at tending the land. Pa taught him all that he knew, and Andy read everything the government printing agency had on timber management, as well as a lot of other stuff from the forestry people who had come and gone. To him "management" didn't mean cutting, it meant growing.

The sale of carefully selected timber kept the Hartleys going, but nobody who came into their land to take out timber was allowed to tear up the surrounding forest. Pa set great store by his woods. Andy worshipped his Pa, and his roots in the piney woods were as deep as any of the old hickory or oak trees were. When he said to Beau, "Pa showed me how to do this...," Beau knew that it was Pa's management and teaching, added to Andy's own, that made the land begin to pay them enough to live comfortably.

The older Hartley often told how Pa saw the end

of the trade in pelts in this country long before anyone else realized that the fur-bearing animals were
almost trapped out. He turned his thought to timber
while the other backwoodsmen were still trudging
cold, wet miles of trap-line for small or nonexistent
returns. Pa went to work for a peckerwood logger, a
one-truck man who took small timbering jobs. He
stayed with his job until he learned some of the
things he needed to know. Then he went to work for
a big sawmill. Pa always kept his eyes open. He
talked with the professional conservationists who
worked for the mill, and he found he could respect
them. He took them hunting on his land, and learned
all he could from them.

When the Sabine National Forest was formed,
Pa hadn't signed his land into it. Still, it butted right
up against their property lines on all sides but one,
and he had always been friends with the rangers in
the forest.

There was never a time when he or Andy, after
him, couldn't call on the head ranger for help or ad-
vice concerning the Hartley timber. They even knew
about the other kinds of land in the big holding, the
grass and the sand hills and the swamp. They
seemed to enjoy working or walking or hunting over
the place, knowing that much of it was just as it had
been when the grant from the king of Spain gave it
to the original Hartley.

From the Sabine River on the east to the state
highway on the west, the land rolled, thick with forest or grassland. There were dozens, maybe hun-
dreds, of small creeks that wandered through shadowy places, never seeing the sun. There were deep
lakes whose bottoms had never been plumbed, there

was the Bog, so fearsome that wild tales about it went back as far as white men went. Some of those tales were true.

So Beau knew how Andy hated to sell even a single tree. The family had to live, and no Hartley would have consented to sell any of the minerals that underlay their home place. Few methods of extraction existed that didn't destroy the surface while it robbed the depths. Because he loved every single tree, Andy had to get some disinterested party to mark the timber for cutting. That was how Chris Garrison came to be his friend.

Chris was an ex-Navy pilot, who flew helicopters in Vietnam. He had more than enough of war and death. When his hitch was up, he returned to the quiet red hills of East Texas to finish his degree in forestry. Once that was in his pocket, he got a job with the Forestry Service and got himself assigned to the Yellowpine District. There his skill with helicopters sent him patrolling the vast reaches of the Angelina and Sabine National Forests.

Andy had been warned about Chris's leg-wound from 'Nam. "Don't walk him to death," Mr. Walker said. He needn't have worried. More often than not, it was Andy's tongue doing the hanging out, at the end of a long day of cruising.

Walking, now that Arthur had sped out of sight, Beau recalled the one time he tried to follow them. The first day they had gone together to mark timber, he felt certain he could keep them in sight. He even managed to do it for a while.

Obviously Chris was impressed by their timber stand. "Why don't you sell some of this hardwood?" he asked. "You have some trees in here, that old wolf walnut, for instance. With those burls, that thing would be worth more than a whole load of pine."

Andy said nothing, but Beau knew he was remembering that Great-Uncle Silas had hung scalps from its branches as a warning to marauding Comanche. After a while, Andy said, "No. We'll just mark the pine this time."

The whistle sounded. As it shrilled through the trees, Beau hurried his steps. The loggers' day had ended. Andy would want a bath and his supper.

Beau wondered if Andy ever regretted staying with the land instead of studying forestry at the college Chris recommended. Maybe if there hadn't been so many young ones to take care of, he might have considered it, or if Ma hadn't gone so quiet and withdrawn after Pa died. She didn't often go to church socials, any more, and she hardly ever visited her few friends. The cheery hat she'd worn to town lived mostly on a shelf in the closet and had for years. She mostly sat or did housework or tended the garden or canned. Her world seemed to end where the trees began.

Many a time the boy watched her sitting on the porch, staring away down the sand road as if waiting. If a strange car should happen to come, she would rise quickly and go into the house. Some time passed before she would come out to greet the newcomers. No, Andy didn't want to leave Ma. That was the main thing.

Now Beau was almost to the clearing. He could hear the big trucks groaning, as they pulled their heavy loads of logs through the sand. The loggers shut off their loaders and skidders after loading the last of the trucks. They would scatter to their variety of battered cars and pickups. He could hear their raucous farewells, full of insulting references to different ones' anatomies and ancestry. Doors slammed, echoing like pistol shots through the forest. Before any of the vehicles could reach him, Beau faded into the thickets and slipped quietly up to the side of the clearing.

Andy was marking on the clipboard he kept his log tallies on. He glanced up toward the thicket where Beau was hiding. The boy ducked. Andy was now moving casually toward the jeep. As he passed a clump of sumac he suddenly disappeared from sight. The game was on.

Each tried to be completely silent, as they circled and hid and sought an advantage. Arthur was there, too, Beau knew, but he hadn't any idea where. Rising from the place where Andy might have spotted him, he caught a low-hanging limb of walnut and snaked along it to wait for developments. Andy came into sight, slipping through the brush with hardly a sound. A quiver of branches told Beau that Arthur was converging on the spot, too. When Andy was directly below, Beau dropped onto his back with a yell. Arthur shouted and rushed in.

The two of them had worked up a pretty good strategy against Andy's long reach, greater weight, and superior strength. Arthur, persistent as barnacles or poison ivy, grabbed one leg and hung on. No amount of pounding or rolling through brush could dislodge him. Beau thought he looked like a loggerhead turtle, his eyes squeezed shut, teeth gritted, never loosing his grip. Once Arthur got his hold, Andy might as well give up.

Beau was almost as tall as Andy, though far lighter. In a wrestling match they weren't too badly out of balance. Andy had taught the younger boy how to use his fists, sparring with both of them. He had never so much as bruised either of the younger boys. He didn't now, as they pulled him down and sat on him. He spit out a mouthful of sand before he cried, "Uncle!" Then they all relaxed in a tumble, laughing.

"You got me this time," Andy said, still spitting sand.

"And last time and next time!" Arthur shouted, his face flushed with triumph.

Beau straightened to hug his knees. "You're slowing down. Must be old age, Big Brother."

"Old," agreed Arthur, nodding wisely.

Andy pulled them both down and hugged them fiercely. Then he pushed them upward and stood himself. "Who's going to drive the old man today?" he asked, dusting his pants and shirt until a fine mist of sand hung about him.

They looked up eagerly. They loved to drive the jeep and were quite competent at driving in the woods, even though Arthur had to stretch himself to reach the foot pedals and see over the hood at the same time. Beau drove often in the woods and on the logging roads. He wasn't old enough to get a license, so he'd never driven in town. Both the boys eagerly wanted to do the driving, but they held themselves in and didn't beg.

Andy bent and picked a green walnut from the ground, holding it behind him. "Which hand?" he asked.

Arthur picked first and got the empty hand.

With a whoop, Beau made two big jumps and landed behind the wheel.

Arthur scrambled into the rear seat, and Andy crawled into the passenger seat and leaned back with a sigh. The short leg-room and the hard seat didn't help much for relaxing, but he hitched around and looked at Beau.

"It's Friday. What say we go out for a little hunt tomorrow?"

"Hunting what?" asked Beau, knowing that all the seasons were now closed.

"Targets of opportunity," Andy said, grinning. "I don't think Chris would miss an old buck squirrel, if we just happened to hit one by accident. For the pot."

"Can I take the fourteen-gauge?" Arthur never failed to ask for that noisy little shotgun.

"For squirrels? Then you'll have to clean 'em," Andy replied, "and eat 'em too, complete with a barrel of toothpicks for getting the shot out of your teeth."

"Aww." Arthur rested his sharp chin on Andy's shoulder. "I suppose the Winchester would do."

"We'll take both of them." Andy reached back, brushing Beau's shoulder with his elbow, and rumpled the boy's hair. "What we're really going after is a bit of target practice."

Beau was concentrating on the bumpy road, with its treacherous patches of deep sand. Even this early in the spring some of the pockets were deep and powdery. He could remember a time when he, too, had been eager to prove himself capable of handling the shotgun. Every trip into the woods had been an adventure. That was the only bad thing about becoming a dead-shot with all the guns, some of the excitement went out of the expeditions. Even Pa's ugly, hard-kicking .45 held no challenge any more, though it had seen use in the First World War, from which Grandpa had brought it home as a souvenir. That was one thing Arthur hadn't got to yet.

Beau looked sideways at Andy, feeling that this was a good a time as he would find. "I got a licking in school today," he said.

Andy's head came up, and his eyebrows quirked. "Oh?"

"For fighting."

"Over what?"

"Gaitor Morfew's got a big, ugly mouth to match the rest of him."

Andy waited for more explanation. When nothing else came, he said, with deceptive mildness, "Don't you ever fight anyone your own size?"

Arthur butted in with, "NO! But Beau would have won, if Mr. Andrews hadn't got there so quick."

"You were fighting over something Gaitor said about me," Andy said. It wasn't a question.

Beau nodded.

Andy gazed off up the track. "Folks who know me, who're my friends, know I'm no thief. Know that no Hartley ever was a thief. What the others think isn't important. Especially bullies and low-lifes like the Morfews. I don't want you fighting over me, you hear me?"

"I just can't stand the likes of Gaitor bad-mouthing you, when his own Pa's a bootlegger, or worse. Taintor has already been in jail a couple of times for fighting and being drunk. Gaitor's got no

41

right to call names."

"That's the kind that always does, Beau. Think about it. Good people aren't bothered that others are good, too. They don't see evil in everything that crosses the road. A bad person? Why he sees nastiness everywhere he looks. Partly because that's the way he is, and partly because when he stands up beside a good man, he looks just as dirty as he is. He'd like to think that everybody was just as crooked and lying and cheating as he is. Makes him more comfortable if he can drag everybody through the mud until nobody can tell who is which."

"Mrs. Terry said something like that," Beau said, whipping the jeep around a sand-pit that was hiding itself in a deep pool of shadow. They drove on, silent. The wood had gone quiet with its before-dark stillness, and the breeze in the jeep was chillier than ever. The road gave way to a graveled county road, one of the two that cut across their property. They followed the dust of the winding track for a bit and then turned into the white sand road with the stone finished ditches that led back to their home ground. Beau drove the jeep straight into the shed beside the red three-quarter-ton pickup. He noted with pleasure that Louise's blue Mustang was already in its slot. She was home early from her teaching job over in Colton.

Arthur hopped out before the jeep had stopped completely. Andy made a grab for him, but he was gone, leaving behind him a helpful comment: "Beau got three licks."

Andy looked at Beau. Beau sighed and climbed out of the jeep. He knew that Andy would rather forget the incident entirely, but a Hartley promise was a promise, indeed. Andy took down the paddle that Pa had made to use on his three oldest, long years before.

Beau bent over yet again, and his brother gave him three light but stinging whacks.

"Now I ain't mad, Beau, but I don't want you fighting at school. Decent folks don't fight. Pa never put up with that kind of thing, and I don't intend to either."

Beau rubbed his seat. The slaps hadn't really hurt, had been much lighter than he had expected, in fact.

"I ain't going to promise," he said.

Andy looked down at him, and laugh-wrinkles appeared around his eyes. "Don't say 'ain't' in front of your sister. Don't they never teach you kids nothing at school?" He whacked Beau on the shoulder with a loosely balled fist.

The two laughed quietly as they went through the dusk into the circle of light on the front porch.

CHAPTER FOUR

Their baby sister, Violet, met them at the door. She was, as usual, dragging Snuggles, her teddy bear, by one almost-furless leg. She held up her arms to Andy to be picked up, though she was really too big for that, now.

"Chris is coming for supper," she announced. She loved having good news when her brothers came home.

Andy swung her high, then gave her a hug before setting her down again. "That's good, Blossom."

"Blossom's a skunk," she giggled.

"You're my stinky little sister," Andy teased, reaching down to pinch Snuggles' flattened nose.

They left her singing, "Stinky brother! Stinky brother!" as she followed them toward the kitchen.

Beau washed his hands in the sink, dried them on the dishtowel, and reached into the cookie jar for one of the fresh raisin cookies that seemed to sprout there regularly.

Louise came in from the back porch and looked at him, hard. Her dark-red hair glowed in the light from the wagon-wheel fixture in the ceiling. "Beau, don't wash your hands in the sink, and don't dry them on the dish towel."

He grinned at his grown sister, retreating to the stool behind the wood stove, where he could eat his cookie in peace. Louise was almost old enough to be his mother, and she sounded as if she were, most of the time.

Andy was always happy when weekends came and she could come home from her teaching job at Colton. He swept her up in a bear-hug, in spite of her protests. Then put her down and turned to wash his own hands in the sink.

Louise threw her hands high in resignation and handed him the dish towel to dry on. "We'll never civilize you two," she sighed. "Ma's tried for years and years, and now I've been putting my back into the job for years more. You're just determined to be woods-footed stump-thumpers, in spite of all. I wish you'd take a leaf out of Chris's book. He can love the woods and still act civilized around the house."

Andy glanced at her teasingly. "How am I going to stand losing both my sisters to the Forest Service?"

Louise grinned, though she blushed slightly. "Violet's got a better claim staked than I have. When she and Chris get together, I can't get a word in edgewise."

Beau giggled from his corner. "Yeah, but you get to stay up later."

Louise turned to flick him with the corner of the dish towel. Her aim was off, because she was laughing so hard, and she punished the stove more than she did her unruly brother.

Andy leaned against the doorframe, weak with laughter. When he sobered a bit, he said, "Louise, before you two slip off together, I need to talk to Chris. Tonight, if possible."

Her face grew grave at once. "About the timber pirating?"

"It's getting pretty serious. More serious than timber pirating, actually. The sheriff came by again this week. Asked me a lot of questions that showed me he really does think I'm involved in this thing. He thinks he's mighty foxy. Asks trick questions, out of the blue, as if he expects me to fall into a trap. If he could find anything at all to back him up, he'd arrest me."

"Andy! Could he?"

"Not on the pitiful little bit of evidence he has, but he's trying as hard as he can to find more. If Chris and Farris Palmer and a lot of Pa's friends weren't standing by me, I'd be looking out through bars right now."

Louise suddenly had tears in her eyes. Her nose grew faintly pink, as it did when she was upset. "Don't talk like that. Surely he couldn't arrest you without sound proof, and there isn't any. They can't create evidence out of nothing."

Andy put his arm about her shoulders and hugged her again. "He could, if only for questioning. I don't think he will, because a man with thousands of acres to tend to isn't going to skip out of the country to escape him. So for now, I think I'm safe. I do need to talk to Chris, see what we can find out about what's really happening, if the sheriff insists on wasting his time watching me." He cocked his head and sniffed, changing the subject. "What's for supper?"

She dabbed a quick kiss on his cheek and moved

away toward the stove. "Cold cabbage and corn pone," she said, wiping her eyes on a corner of the now-limp dishtowel.

Andy chuckled. "Then it'll be the first time ever Chris got cold cabbage!"

Beau noticed the emphasis on Chris. He, too, chuckled, calling unwelcome attention to himself. Louise shooed both of them out of the kitchen with the popping end of the dishtowel.

"He'd better get used to it. It won't be the last he gets," she snapped after them.

The two fled onto the back porch, where Ma was sitting in the darkness, her handwork forgotten on her lap. She was watching the last stain of red fade behind the pines to the west A wisp of cirrus cloud, very high, had caught the last brightness of the sunset and held it, pink and gold, above the dark shapes of the trees.

When the last of the color had drained away, Andy stooped to kiss Ma's cheek. "How's my best girl tonight?" he asked.

She smiled, turning her face so the light from the kitchen window caught her hair as a mist of silver. "You look tired," she said, reaching up to lay her hand over his, still on her shoulder. "Have the cutters finished?"

"Not by a long shot," Andy replied. "It takes a while, when I stand over them to make certain they don't tear up the young stuff or cut anything they don't have to. You ought to see those fellows when I make 'em clean up the brush tops before moving on to another cutting site. They never heard of such a thing."

"I know. Your Pa used to keep his cutting sites

47

as neat as most people's houses. Nobody could understand why, until a few had fires in their cut-over timber. Then they could see the good sense in keeping a lot of dry kindling-wood out of their woods. Not many took the trouble to do that."

Beau, startled at his mother's mention of Pa, leaned against her shoulder. "I got a licking in school, today," he said to break the sudden awkward silence.

She turned her head, her face now shadowed. "Somebody talking about Andy." It was no question. Ma had ways of knowing things, even if she didn't go out much now.

Beau perched on the side of her chair to tell her about it. He didn't mention the second licking from Andy. That went without saying. He could see that she understood exactly why he had felt compelled to tie into Gaitor Morfew.

They were still talking about it when Chris's car came winding through the woods, casting its twin beams of light across the trees as it came. They could hear Violet's squeal of delight from inside the house, then the bang of the front door screen as she rushed to greet her favorite.

Andy pulled his mother to her feet and offered her his arm. They went into the front of the house, as Beau stopped in the kitchen to help Louise put the meal on the table. In a minute, Chris came to stand in the doorway, with Violet draped around his neck, clinging to him possessively.

The cold cabbage and cornpone that Louise had threatened had magically changed into fresh early turnip greens, roast pork done to a crisp brown that only Ma and her woodstove could achieve, and hot, fluffy cornbread. The rice stood, each grain a masterpiece of fluffiness, just waiting for the rich brown gravy from the pork. Apple pies flanked the table, along with a lemon meringue, made especially for Chris.

Andy said the blessing while they all held hands around the table. Beau didn't wonder that the blessing seemed more fervently thankful than usual. Such a feast called for thankfulness.

When justice had been done to the meal, Chris and Andy took their heavy mugs of black, chickoried coffee onto the front porch, where light from the front room gave illumination through the many windowpanes. Beau slipped out behind them and moved into a shadowy corner, where he wouldn't be noticed.

The whippoorwills, early this year, were fluttering their calls through the night. An occasional owl hooted as it went about its hunting. The silence was companionable for a while, but there was an edge of unease. Beau could feel it quite plainly.

Chris spoke, at last. "Louise says the sheriff has questioned you again."

Andy sighed and set his cup on Ma's fern-stand. He leaned his splint-bottomed chair against the wall, and the light from the window cut him neatly in half.

"He still thinks it's my truck taking out those logs. He says the tire tracks match. But, Lord, I run Firestones. Half the trucks in the county have that tread."

"Andy, did you ever think that it might be one of your trucks?"

"Just what do you mean?" When Andy's voice

got that quiet, Beau knew a person'd better look out. Beau sat still and silent, waiting for the answer.

"Where's your big truck tonight?"

"Loaded and down at the railroad yards, I suppose. Deke Phillips loaded it and drove it in this afternoon. He'll have it back by tomorrow. No, it's Friday. He won't bring it back until Monday."

Chris set his cup beside Andy's and bent forward, full into the light. "Is it possible that he might unload it early and drive it into the woods for an illegal haul tonight? Think about that for a minute."

Andy was silent for a long moment. "Loading logs and unloading them takes a long time. Particularly for a tired man. Deke is too trifling to work overtime, even for mighty good money."

Chris didn't argue, but he looked skeptical.

"Where did they take timber from this time?" Andy asked.

"Yellowpine District. Way off at the back. They took about thirteen acres. Stripped off the pole pine clean as a whistle, all prime stuff, like the rest they've stolen. Cut, stripped, loaded, and hauled before anybody had an inkling it was being done. There must have been fifteen or twenty loads."

"Who found it?"

"I did. Spotted it from the chopper. They cut it a little closer than usual, this time. I could see bare-looking spots where there hadn't been any ninety days ago. Radioed in, got Walker, and he had the sheriff meet me. I took him right over the spot, him and the federal marshal. The cut was altogether on government land."

"Did either of them mention me?"

Chris shook his head. "The sheriff wouldn't say

anything to me, anyway. he knows where I stand on that. I don't think the marshal is quite so uptight about you as the sheriff is."

"Well, I wish he'd quit saying anything to me, too." Andy's grin held little humor. "Almost seems as if somebody's trying to sic him onto me, doesn't it? If he ever finds anything, equipment or whatever, on one of the locations that might ever have belonged to me, I'm a dead duck. You know that I've bought and sold and traded trucks and loaders and skidders and trailers all over this area for years, and Pa before me. Half the stuff in use in the woods around here has been through our hands at one time or another."

"Well, you certainly don't need to steal. You've got timber enough to get rich on, if you'd cut it. Nobody can say you're in any kind of desperate bind for money. Only the fact that you're madly in love with all your trees keeps you from mopping up, money-wise." Chris was chuckling, but what he said was quite true.

Andy set the front legs of his chair down squarely, with a thump. "Well, we're not hurting. Everybody has to have something coming in regularly, and we do, though not in amounts that somebody like Ralls might think was enough for a family our size. He doesn't know anything about us. He seems to think that because we live so far back in the woods and don't socialize and join the Lions Club and such that we're redneck trash, ripe for anything crooked that comes along. I guess he doesn't know many people who don't owe a dime. Takes less if you don't owe any money."

"Andy, you don't have to live back here like

poor folks." Chris's voice was tentative.

"Do we seem like really poor folks to you?" Andy's voice held a hint of anger.

"Of course not. But your mother, wouldn't she be more comfortable in town?"

"Comfortable? What would she have there that she hasn't here? We have lights, indoor plumbing, TV, a deep freeze, butane stove, if Ma'd ever use it instead of the old wood-burner. We have the quiet, and the trees. Clean air. Squirrels in the yard. Nobody running up our front steps every five minutes. We have what the city people are always running out here to find, but in our case we have it all the time, right outside our doors. Besides, Ma would go crazy in town, with no trees to watch. They're what she has left of Pa."

Chris raised his hands in a defensive position. "Whoa, whoa! Remember me? I'm a woods boy, too. I'm convinced. It's just that some people don't think that way."

Andy relaxed. The window-light marked out his grin. "If nothing else, you've made me count my blessings."

The creak of the screen door made Beau jump in his dark corner. There was a soft pad of footsteps and a soft grunt, as Violet's weight landed in Chris's lap.

"Gently, Sweet Pea. Take it easy on the old man."

She giggled, rooting her head into his shoulder. "Andy called me 'Stinky'!"

"That's because he has to live with you all the time. I just visit, when you're on your good behavior," Chris smoothed her tumbled hair.

"Well, why don't you come to live with us, too? Then you could call me 'Stinky,' and I wouldn't even mind."

He chuckled. "You keep asking Louise that. Just tell her to set the day. Now be still. I'm talking to Andy."

Violet subsided, snuggling down into his lap, and was silent as Chris rocked gently in the high-backed old rocking chair he always chose to sit in. Beau, in his corner, felt a twinge. He always felt it when anything was said about Chris and Louise. He wasn't ready to give her up yet, even to anyone as nice as Chris.

"Where do you suppose they're selling the poles, Chris?" Andy asked. "Only a couple of places anywhere close by could possibly handle them, and I don't think either of those would buy stolen stuff."

Chris grunted. "The sheriff has checked out every possible buyer for ten counties around. I think he even has informers double-checking for him. Once he finds out who's doing the buying, it won't be any problem to find who's selling."

Ma and Louise, done with the dishes, joined them on the porch, though it was chilly in the spring night. The freshness of the pine-scented woods was sharp, and birdcalls and cricket-fiddlings and a frog chorus from the creek made a few goose-pimples worth while. They listened quietly, talked a bit of logs and weather and world troubles. Not timber pirates. They weren't discussed in front of Ma. She knew, of course, as she knew many things people tried to keep from her. Still, not in front of Ma.

Andy rose and stretched. "While you were sitting in the sky, doing nothing, I was working my tail feathers off. Time I got to bed. Beau, you, too. Bedtime."

Beau stirred, stretching his legs, then came out of his corner, as Andy lifted the sleeping Violet from Chris's lap and took her into the house. Ma came close behind them. Louise stayed on the porch with Chris.

Beau lay listening to the night sounds long after the others had settled for the night, long after Chris's pickup had muttered away down the road, and Louise's heels had tapped their way to her room. In the nearby wood an owl caught a mouse. Its shrill squeak was perfectly audible. A screech owl's call trembled through the trees, making the chickens murmur restlessly in their tight wire pen. Armadillos rattled the armor-plate of their backs along the rough siding of the car shed, making their way to the salt blocks Andy kept there for them.

Old Maggie growled, deep in her throat, threatening to bark but not quite waking enough to do it. The faintest of skunk-scent drifted into the house. Beau smiled into the darkness. Even in her sleep, Maggie hated a skunk.

Far away toward the bottomlands, a hound bellowed. Another took up the cry. It wasn't hunting season. Those were dogs hunting on their own, keeping their noses sharp. Maggie's pup, Rooster, took off from the back porch. His deep roar was soon joined with the voices of the others.

Beau gritted his teeth. They were running a deer, he knew. Rooster was a hunting fool, and if he didn't take care he was going to ruin himself for a coon dog.

Maggie woke and grumbled at the distant run.

Her old legs couldn't carry her as they had in the old days, but her heart wanted desperately to go with the others. She whined until Beau heard Andy say, "Shut up, Maggie. I hear 'em."

She whimpered. Beau heard her toenails scrape against the side of the house as she stood up to put her nose to the window. When her snuffled query brought no response from her master, she turned around three times, as if he could see her doing it, in the hole she had dug in the flowerbed and settled for the night.

Beau turned over and pulled the covers higher. Maggie must have had it easy when she was young, he thought. She had been Pa's dog. Followed him everywhere through the woods, with Andy right behind her. When Pa had died, she had mourned for weeks, staying in the swamp where he'd died. She had come in at last, thin and weak and covered with ticks.

The whole family had nursed her, after Andy bathed her and poured warm milk and raw eggs down her throat. At last the bones were covered once more by flesh, and the luster touched her fur. Her eyes got a little of their old shine back, though never as much as before. After that she became Andy's dog. Then it was Beau who followed her whip-like tail.

Andy was seventeen when he became the head of the household. For the first time, Beau wondered if that hadn't been awfully scary. He remembered that there had been talk of Andy's going to college, but that had been pushed back out of sight, and Andy hadn't mentioned it ever again until Chris brought up the subject. Only once in a while, deep in the woods with his brothers, had he said anything that might make Beau think he still thought of college.

Lying there in the sturdy house Beau wondered about things. Was there anything he could do? He wished there was. Something that would clear Andy of suspicion. Something that would help him go to college, even now that he was grown. Something that would make it so he wouldn't have to cut the trees he loved so much in order to keep the family going.

Beau had learned from his brother to think of the trees as giants who had weathered storms and fire and insects for more years than any three or four men could tally. When the saw touched them, they shivered as if they knew what was coming. An enemy they couldn't resist was attacking. Only man was a pest they couldn't survive. As the saw bit in, their tops began to whip back and forth, as if the tree were in agony. Finally, with a terrible scream and a crackling of wood, the tree would crash to the earth, sending showers of needles and cones and bark and broken branches out in a wide arc around it. There seemed to be a deep sigh, as all the surrounding trees whipped back from the draft of wind.

The last thought in Beau's mind, as he drifted off to sleep was the crashing of mighty trees.

CHAPTER FIVE

Turbo Morfew's world became uncertain and confused with the loss of his land and his beloved trees. If his long-suffering wife Sadie had lived to ease him over the change, things might have been better. But she finished the dishes one night, emptied the wash pan of water into the back yard, said, "Oh, my goodness!" and died. Just like that.

That left Turbo, who had seldom done more than grunt at his two sons, to raise them alone. No sooner had Sadie fallen than he caught her up to go for help. There was no life in that over-light body. He had stood there, dry-eyed, and sworn a mighty oath to her unhearing ears.

"I'll raise them boys so good—you'll see, Sadie. They'll go all the way through school, too. I know I argued with you about that, but you set such a store by schooling, I'll see they go iffen I have to beat 'em black and blue. And they'll be well-spoke, too. No sassing their elders."

The boys themselves, standing, bewildered, while their father talked, hadn't understood for a while exactly what his words meant. They had, after all, been only five and nine years old, at the time.

Their lives had changed drastically, then. No

sooner was their mother decently buried than the government surveyors descended on their land, marking out lines through the deepest of the forest. For two years their father was so harassed and miserable with trying to hold onto his land that he had little time to worry about the boys.

That had been fine with them. Taintor was in school, and Turbo saw that he set off for the school bus stop a mile away every morning. He never thought to check that he made it all the way. So Taintor often peeled off into the woods, stashed his books in a hollow tree, and waited for his young brother to join him for a day of rambling, creek-fishing, or playing in the forest. Not always, of course. Mostly he went to school and sat through six hours of bleary-eyed boredom.

At the end of two years, when Gaitor was about to finish the first grade, the big move came. Turbo set the two to work as if they had been adults, and they, being well-grown for their ages and strong with country-boy muscles, pitched in and helped him move the house and the chimney, all the livestock, and the poultry to their new location.

Once the father's attention was no longer focused on his battle with the government, it turned to his sons. Obviously, his word to Sadie wasn't being kept right to the letter. While they set off for school every day, he soon found that they frequently didn't arrive there at all. He began a system of beatings and cursings that didn't do much good. Then he personally, drunk or sober, took them out to wait for the bus, saw them safely aboard, and watched them out of sight. That did the trick.

Making them polite was another matter. He was

an uncouth man, himself, and he wouldn't have recognized really courteous behavior. He knocked the
worst cuss-words back into their teeth. All in all, he
did the best that he could manage. The fact that he
slipped deeper and deeper into an alcoholic fog
hadn't improved matters much, either. The world of
the sand hills was one he scorned, and his old world,
the deep places of the forest, was gone with the
creatures it supported. He was left stranded in an
alien place with no refuge and no comfort left to
him.

His world got dimmer and dimmer, as he
drowned it in drink. Once Taintor finished his
schooling, one month before his nineteenth birth-
day, Turbo began to relax his hold on the boys. His
store of energy for such purposes was just about exhausted, anyway, and he felt that as Taintor had finished, then Gaitor would naturally do the same. The
times he had to sober up and wash and shave in order to go into town and confer with the principal
about Gaitor's misbehavior were a lot of bother, but
he managed, mostly. He never guessed his younger
son had become a bully.

Part of his inborn creed was that boys fought,
the way men fought. That was man-nature. Sometimes they fought pretty bloody, too, but no real
man (or boy either) would pick on someone smaller.
Turbo would have been distressed terribly, if he had
known the reputation Gaitor was building among
the younger children in the school. Yet if he had
known, he would only have beaten the boy harder
and more often, and that, in turn, would have trig-
gered more bullying.

The days flowed by, interrupted by the comings

and goings of his sons, the infrequent baying of old Pastor, who sometimes took a notion to run coon or possums. Some days were worse than others. Those were the days when he talked to Sadie, feeling, somehow, that she still could hear and might care about his pain.

Turbo didn't know when Gaitor was expelled from school, for the time never came when the boys felt easy about telling him. Instead, they kept to a schedule that looked much the same as before.

The old man did a bit of cooking for his sons. He ran the ragged broom over the floor once in a while, when the trash got too deep. Once he set a mousetrap, but he never remembered to check it, and the mouse it caught mummified behind the wood box. Turbo Morfew tried. Nobody could deny that. Too bad that he couldn't succeed.

CHAPTER SIX

Beau shivered. Even the heavy plaid mackinaw Andy insisted he wear hadn't turned all of the spring-dawn chill.

Arthur and Andy were hunkered down with him at the base of a huge sweet gum that two of them could have barely reached around. They were cold, too. Beau could feel Arthur shivering against his side, as he snuggled between the two larger brothers for warmth. Even in summer these woods didn't get really hot. The ground was low and damp, no matter what sort of dry weather went on round-about.

These woods edged the swamp, with the Bog in the middle. That was a place the younger boys never approached in their roamings through the Hartley forest. The swamp held memories that were too tragic, too fearsome, to mess with. They often hunted deer or squirrel out here in the hardwood stand on the edge, but where the ground began to get soft and trembly underfoot they stopped. All kinds of small game abounded among the oaks and hickories; their nuts drew them like a magnet, but, as did the boys, the animals feared the bog. Only the high-springing gray squirrels, the flying-squirrels, and the birds dared its depths. The ground-walkers kept away unless hard-pressed by some predator.

Mist hung over the wood almost always. Now the first light caught it into a net of pink and gold. The tops of the trees seemed suspended like islands above the low-lying sea of mist. Sky islands, but they stood steady in the still morning, while the mist swirled about them. Sometimes it revealed an entire tree for a fleeting instant. Sometimes the fog hid everything for a long moment, before the breeze moved it again.

Gradually, the trees came into sight, first as dark shapes, flat gray on white. Then as rounded ones, standing away from the pale swirls. At last they were clearly visible as trees, each with its own character and personality. Beau knew them as individuals, as did Andy, as had their Pa.

With the coming of the light, the squirrels began to move. The brothers watched, whispering softly, as they observed the paths the perky rodents chose through the treetops. They knew that squirrels, much as did people, stuck to familiar routes, following them regularly for as long as they lived, or until the trees that were their highways were cut down.

By watching them, learning their routes now, the Hartleys could assure themselves of many easy kills, once the hunting season opened in the fall. Not that they killed many from any one location, and not that they killed for sport. One reason it took little money for them to live was the good store of squirrel and fish and venison in Ma's freezer. Enough to last the year around, without buying the tasteless, expensive stuff at the market in town.

Once the sun was well up, the mist lifted and dissipated among the tree trunks, they took their guns from the jeep and put their jackets, unnecessary now, in the back. Andy set up targets, chips of wood tacked to thick tree boles, single leaves pinned with a thorn to a town-ant colony that rose half his height from the reddish soil. They shot for over an hour, until they used the carefully allotted amount of ammunition each had brought.

When the guns were back into their cases and stashed in the jeep, Andy looked down at the two. "Let's walk," he said, heading out through the underbrush. As Beau followed, he found a moment to regret that Maggie wasn't here. She still loved, aching legs and all, to follow Andy through the woods.

Beau loved these times, himself. Best of all times, he thought. He always took the tail-end position, last in line. That way he could stop to look at bright orange fungi, thrusting up through the dead leaves, or at the mist-hung web of a cotton spider, sitting in her yellow-and-green finery, waiting at the center of a geometrical trap. He could see everything and not have his heels stepped on by a complaining Arthur.

From the tail of his eye he saw motion and stopped again. A slender wasp, tiny and quick, dropped suddenly from the sky, dive-bombing the spider's vulnerable under side. The spider seemed to realize the danger and flung herself toward the ground below her, but she made a fatal mistake. She left her thread-line attached to the web, instead of dropping freely. It left her swinging, just short of the ground. The small wasp pounced, thrusting its poison-laden stinger again and again into the helpless spider.

In only moments, the spider dropped slowly to

the ground, her silk unreeling from her spinnerets, even though she was unconscious. The prey was too large for the wasp to carry away. As Beau stepped away after his brothers, he saw her tugging at the spider, which was more than twice her size. She moved it toward a fallen twig, over it, toward her hole in the ground. As she bore her prey to the place she had made for her eggs, she hummed happily, a high-pitched droning song.

He thought of Pa's old saying: "A woman who sings at her work makes a happy man." Beau wondered if wasp husbands were happy.

Andy had called a couple of times and was waiting with Arthur, bent over some tiny plants, when Beau caught up with him.

"Looky," Arthur said, pushing aside some dead leaves. Beau bent, too, and looked. Four sun-dew plants spread their hungry mouths, there in the mulch of the woods-floor. Beau shivered. He had read stories of terrible cannibal plants in the jungle—man-eaters. These were so much the same. Just infinitely smaller. They could catch and devour mosquitoes and ants and gnats. Beau lifted his foot to squash them, but Andy caught him.

"Don't!" he said.

"Ugh! Why not? They're ugly, and they eat things."

"Eat things? Why, Beau, you eat things. Everything has to eat something. The big pine over there has to eat to live. So does the catbird up there looking at us as if we were three tomcats. We all have to eat, it's how we live."

"But they catch 'em alive, Andy. And they're slimy."

"Sticky." Arthur corrected him. He put out a finger and touched one, very lightly. "Not a bit slimy."

Andy looked troubled, and Beau sighed. He was in for a lesson, which wasn't a bad thing. Ordinarily he enjoyed learning everything Andy had to teach about the forest things, but it was almost time for breakfast. His stomach told him that as accurately as did the angle of the sun through the trees. He hoped this lesson would be a short one.

"Just wait and watch for a bit, boys," Andy said, putting a moccasined foot on either side of the cluster of sun-dews. He leaned a bit, staring downward. Beau and Arthur bent, too, their eyes intent. Beau's stomach growled softly. Dumb sun-dews, he thought. Here I am starving to death, and we have to watch a bunch of plants. But he kept silent, anyway, watching.

They weren't really ugly, he realized. The "mouth" was like two cupped hands, brought together to catch water from a spring. They were palest creamy gold, down in the hinges, darkening to pale green as it got nearer the edge. Around the rim was a line of deep pink. All along the rim stood little pink eyelash-like hairs, each one with a drop of moisture at its tip. When a beam of light managed to make its way through the trees, the drops glistened.

The woods were very still. Only the scrabbling of the squirrels above broke the silence. Gnats swarmed about the boys, becoming bolder and bolder. At last Beau became so annoyed that he swatted one down. It hit the soft ground, got up, and flew unsteadily in circles, finally settling onto the inviting cushion of the sun-dew. The tiny hairs quivered at its touch. In about two heartbeats, the little hinge pulled the sides of the mouth together. The gnat was gone, enfolded in the sun-dew's trap. That plant remained closed, and the others waited patiently.

Andy spoke softly. "What did you see?"

Beau was always uncomfortable when Andy looked straight into him, probing his thoughts with those blue eyes.

Beau shrugged. "Saw it eat a gnat."

"What else?"

"I knocked the gnat down, to begin with, if that's what you mean."

"No, that's not what I mean. What was the gnat doing?"

"Just sitting there, drinking in the dew, I guess. Till the walls closed in on him."

"You reckon he hurt much, when he was caught?"

"Well...no. He didn't even try to get away. He just sat there."

"I've noticed that, too," Andy said. "Sometimes insects struggle, and the sticky dew holds them tight, but the things that taste the juice don't ever try to escape. They don't seem to feel anything. I think it's something like a drug. Anesthesia."

"So they don't mind getting eaten?"

"Something like that. You know, I kind of admire those little sun-dews. Think of the old pine, now, a tree more than two hundred years old. The Hartleys have owned it for that long, and no telling how much older than that it is. In all that time, it hasn't stirred a peg to help itself. Just drinks the water and minerals out of the ground, reaches up for the sun on its needles to make its food. Almost all the plants are the same. They just take what comes. Not this little fellow. He takes mighty little out of the soil. Mainly water. He's not much bigger than your thumb, but he stands up here and catches his own dinner. Anything from a deer to a bobcat could squash him flat without noticing it, but he asks nothing from anybody except a fair chance."

Beau couldn't think of anything to say, so he kept his eyes fixed on the plants. A big army ant marched into view. He saw the sun-dew and stopped, but his good sense got him moving again, past the plants. Then something else, hunger or greed, sent him back again. He stood up on his hind legs and peered over the lip of the mouth of one. The pink hairs were very still, the dew on them glistening invitingly. The ant waved his feelers about, sensing after danger that his instinct told him was there. Hunger, or whatever it was, got the better of him.

He put his front legs on the lip. It tipped down obligingly beneath his weight. He reached over with his sharp cutting jaws to nip off a bit of the sun-dew. When he tried to draw back he was caught by the sticky hairs. He scrabbled his back feet, which were still on the ground. For an instant it seemed that he might just get away, but the sun-dew gave him no chance. The other lip came over quickly, closing. At last the back legs of the ant disappeared beneath a fringe of pink.

Andy stood up. "See?" he asked.

Then he led off through the woods again, and Beau took a last look backward. Two of the sun-dews were tightly closed, digesting their meals. Two were still waiting patiently for their breakfasts.

Andy circled wide around the Bog. Beau often wished his brother would lead them into it. Andy knew the ways, as Pa had done. Many past refusals told him that today would be no different. If he ever learned the paths through the Bog, he supposed that it would have to be on his own. Still, he thought he'd wait until Arthur was a little older. Then they'd go together. They circled widely, leaving the area of the Bog to go through thick stands of pine. They passed the spot where the loggers were working, moving beyond it toward the north boundary. There Andy stopped so quickly that Arthur bumped his back.

"Listen!"

The boys stood silent, straining their ears. At first Beau could hear nothing except the silence and the thumping of his own heart. His ears had been set to tune out Arthur's constant chattering. Gradually his hearing attuned itself to the woods' sounds. Buzzing insects, a squirrel barking somewhere away to their left, the whispers of leaves and pine needles. A bird called sharply, a jay, remarking upon their presence. There was also a man-made sound. Someone was sawing.

This wasn't the noisy popping scream of the power saws that the professional loggers used. This was the swinging bite of a two-man crosscut saw. Beau was all too familiar with the sound, for he and Andy had cut many a backlog for Ma's fireplace with Pa's thin-honed crosscut.

He leaned close to Andy. "Who?"

Arthur never fooled around with his questions. He always got right to the point, and he cut in with "Is it the timber pirates, Andy?"

"I wouldn't think so," said Andy, holding up his hand. They heard the tree crack sharply as the weight of the standing timber overbalanced the thin strip of wood still holding it to its roots. Then came the grinding crash as it fell through a crackle of smaller trees surrounding it to thump heavily to the ground. They could feel the vibration of that fall in the ground under their feet.

Andy looked puzzled. "They've gone out of their way to make me look like a thief. Why would they steal off my land now? Doesn't make sense."

Arthur pushed past him. "Let's go see."

Andy grabbed his arm and hauled him back. "No way. You stay here with Beau. Right here. You understand? Don't move a peg! I'll go for a look-see and be right back."

If Andy waited for an argument, he'd have had one from Beau, but before the boy could get his mouth open his older brother disappeared into a thicket of blackhaw and palmetto. He moved like a ghost, and neither boy could hear a single hint of his passage through the forest as he moved away from them. They huddled together, listening with all their energy.

A few minutes went by. They seemed like hours.

"Andy's been gone for a mighty long time," Arthur whispered.

Beau thought it felt that way, too, but he knew it hadn't been that long, and he didn't want to alarm Arthur. "He's just watching them. You wait. He'll be back in a minute or two."

Arthur subsided. He was quiet for some minutes. Then he began to squirm.

"I don't hear anything at all now, Beau. I think they got Andy. I'm scared."

Beau looked down at the child's big eyes staring from his white face. "Don't be silly. Andy can take care of himself. They won't even know he's there." He didn't quite believe his own words, but anything to reassure Arthur.

Now he was listening so hard that he felt as if his ears had stretched out as long as a rabbit's. Nothing. Nothing. Then, suddenly, there came the sound of voices, loud and angry. The boys were too far from them to understand what they were saying.

Beau straightened and reached for Arthur's shoulder. "Come on. Let's go see what's going on," he tugged the younger boy forward.

He didn't have to pull hard. Arthur was already moving, though his eyes were now enormous, his teeth gritted. Beau could feel him quivering beneath his hand, but he didn't hang back. The two boys kept close together, as they slipped through the brush in the direction Andy had taken.

Some distance ahead, a truck started its engine. A door slammed, and it crashed through the brush, roaring down whatever narrow trail it had made in getting into their woods. A second truck roared to life. It evidently had a heavy load, for there was a protesting whine from the engine.

The boys began to run through the thick timber. By the time they broke through the undergrowth into the less-cluttered pine timber the truck was moving swiftly away from them. They caught only glimpse of the second truck as it high-tailed it toward the road. Once it hit the graveled surface, it would gather speed and be gone. The load, Beau could see through the tree trunks, was six choice pines that made a heavy load even for so tough a truck.

Arthur wasn't thinking about trucks. "Andy! Andy!" he called at the top of his voice.

Beau called, too, but he had a sinking feeling that there wouldn't be any reply. And there wasn't. They searched the whole area, meeting at the ends of their circuits, going through the entire part of the wood where the men had cut. Except for piles of brush that were branches on big trees a few hours before, they found nothing.

"Andy, where are you?" they called, once more, almost in unison. No answer. They separated again, going over every inch of the ground. Except for a hole into which Beau went almost up to his knees. Someone had been digging, out in the middle of the woods. Why? There was something funny, different about this stand of woods. Something was missing besides Andy and a few pine trees, but his dazed wits couldn't come up with any answer.

Beau stopped, at last, beside his brother and sighed. "They've taken him." he said. This time he wasn't guessing. "Stay here."

Without waiting for Arthur to argue, he left him in the center of the clearing. As fast as he could move, he tore through the woods. Across the thicket was a long curve, almost a switchback, in the county road. If he could get there in time, he might just catch the truck. He knew it had to go pretty slowly until it hit the graded and graveled surface. Beau didn't stop to think what he would do with the truck, if he caught it. He just ran as fast as his legs could travel over the rough mulch of the woods floor.

Brush whipped at his face. Sawvines and branches tore at his legs and chest, but he ignored those unimportant hurts. He went flying in one leap over small gullies and fallen logs. Once, coming onto an unexpected clear spot, he even sailed over a startled razorback hog, which had been rooting in the dead leaves. The boar gave a protesting squeal, but Beau was almost beyond hearing it by the time it got its wits together.

The bend in the road was almost a mile away. Beau could hear the truck laboring under its load, as it moved almost parallel with him for a time, then bore away to follow the irregular curve of the roadway. He was making a lot of noise as he ran, too. His legs ached, and his chest burned outside with scratches and inside with the effort of pumping breath into his lungs, but he was still running. he had heard of second wind for a runner. He would have liked a bit, just then.

For all his effort, he was just too late. Beau burst into the roadway a moment after the truck had passed. He saw it, just as it was moving onto a straight downhill stretch that would allow it to build up speed. Too much speed. He didn't stop. He ran headlong after it, down the dusty road.

The effort was useless. The truck gained momentum and pulled away in a dusty cloud. He followed until his legs gave out completely, leaving him crumpled into a heap in the middle of the road. his face burned with sweat and tears. He hadn't even succeeded in getting the license number.

Andy was gone. Beau had no way of knowing who took him or why, but he did know how it had been done. He lay in the dirt, pounding his fists into the road.

"If you hurt my brother, I'll get you! I'll find you wherever you go!"

CHAPTER SEVEN

He could still hear the noise of the truck, but it was now out of sight. Beau lay where he had fallen until his breath steadied to a wheeze. When his heart no longer threatened to pound its way out through his ribs or to tear itself to pieces against his backbone, he rolled over and lay staring at the cloudless sky. The Saturday sky.

Where was Andy? Had the thieves truly taken him away with them?

Spurred by the thought, Beau turned onto his stomach and raised himself on quivering arms. His legs were shaking, too, once he stood up on them, but he knew he was strong. He ran for miles every week, just for the joy of the motion. He sawed and chopped wood to keep the wood stove going. He worked in Ma's garden every day of the spring and summer and much of the fall. All those things built leg muscle, but nothing he had ever done had prepared him for the kind of effort that he had just made. He felt as wobbly as a new-born fawn.

There was a rustling in the roadside brush. Beau's heart jumped again, and he leaped for cover. Hidden in a thick stand of huckleberry, he peered out cautiously and laughed. He was careful not to laugh aloud, and he controlled it before he stepped down into the road from his hiding place.

He saw a knotty club of respectable proportions come thrusting through the undergrowth. At its business end a small but determined brown hand was clamped, and another had cautiously spread open a space in the branches just wide enough for peeping through. There was no mistaking Arthur's dark tumble of red-brown hair, shadowing his thin face. Only the pale outline was distinguishable as he looked out and saw his brother standing in the road.

"Beau? That's really you?"

"Sure is. Arthur, you gave me the grandpappy of all scares!"

The younger boy grinned, pleased that he'd been able to startle Beau so much. Then he looked troubled.

"I didn't mean to scare you. Did you catch 'em? did you see Andy?"

Beau sighed, feeling, now, as if he might fall on his face at any moment. "No. To both questions. I was too late. Just seconds too late. If they took Andy, they got away with him. Let's get back to the jeep. I've got to get to a phone and call Chris."

Arthur brightened. "He'll know what to do," he agreed. He pitched his club back into the woods.

Beau led out, trotting down the road as fast as his trembling legs would carry him. Arthur had no trouble, now, in keeping up with him. They cut off the road onto a side trail that was a shortcut, though it went much nearer to the Bog than Beau liked to think about, but it led them to the jeep faster than the road would have done. For once, Arthur neither complained nor chattered. They checked that the guns were still in the back of the jeep, and both climbed into the seats. Arthur took the passenger side without argument or protest. For once, he seemed glad that he was the smaller of the two of them.

The engine started on the first try, and they tore out through the rough tangle of tracks and trails. Beau ignored hummocks and saplings and other obstructions that he usually would have avoided. Today he hadn't time to go around anything that wasn't higher or deeper than the jeep itself. As they jounced through the forest, he told Arthur how near he came to catching the truck.

"And you didn't get the license number?" Arthur sounded disgusted. On TV, the hero always got the license number.

"The truck was too far off. I couldn't see who was driving, either, or who was in the passenger seat. Wrong angle. Chris won't have much to go on. Just a rusty red Ford truck loaded with six big pine logs. Half the trucks in the woods are rusty red Fords."

"Chris will find Andy, Beau. Chris can find anything, if he tries."

* * * * * * *

Chris didn't seem as confident as Arthur, when they called him. He asked a lot of questions, most of which Beau couldn't answer. Then he said, "Stay at the house. Both of you. I'll get the sheriff. We'll be out in about an hour."

Beau was near tears, now. "NO, Chris! You can

find those trucks with the chopper. Can't you go look for him now?"

"Whoa, now, Beau. Calm down. In the first place, I can't just take the 'copter any time I please. It isn't mine, it's the Forest Service's. I just fly it for them. Right now Charlie Riggs is out on patrol over the Angelina. We'll radio him, but by the time he can make it back those trucks could be anywhere at all, or hidden in the thick woods."

"Oh, Chris, what'll we do?" Beau's voice cracked, and he clung to the phone so tightly his knuckles hurt.

"First off, you take hold of yourself and don't scare your mother and sisters to death. You've got to tell them, but not the same way you told me. Keep it cool, don't make it scary. I'll be there as soon as I can. Then we'll go out to the spot where they were cutting and see if we can find anything. Don't worry. Even if they kidnapped Andy, I don't think they'd hurt him. Stealing timber is one thing. Assault is another."

Beau knew that he had been about to say "murder" and had caught himself in time. Now he was calmer and said only, "Okay, if you say so."

"I say so. See you as fast as I can," and Chris was gone. Though Chris had tried his best not to, he had frightened the boy a lot. Those timber pirates had the best of reasons not to want Andy to be able to talk. They might well hurt or kill him to keep him quiet, for he was an eyewitness to their theft. They wouldn't want anyone alive and healthy who could testify against them and break up their profitable trade in stolen timber.

Beau didn't say anything about that to Arthur.

He led his brother into the kitchen. Frightened or not, his stomach was saying that breakfast-time was a long way past. He sliced pork roast thickly and made sandwiches for both. Then they went onto the porch to wait for Chris and the sheriff. He was glad that his mother and sisters had planned to go to Beaumont shopping, this morning. He didn't want to be the one who told Ma Andy had disappeared. Or how he disappeared.

"They went shopping for Violet's Easter dress," Arthur told Chris, as soon as the sheriff's Plymouth rolled to a stop and Chris looked at the empty slot where Louise's car usually stayed.

"Good. Maybe we can get things straightened out before they come back. Then they won't have to worry about it at all." Chris opened the back door and got in with Arthur. "You get into the front, Beau, and show Sheriff Ralls where to go."

While they drove, the two boys were able to give a complete account of the morning, as well as of Andy's disappearance.

"Maybe Andy met some of his friends and went off with them," Sheriff Ralls said in a low voice to Chris. He sounded as if he meant it, and Beau went cold all over.

He turned to look at the big man beside him. "You think we're pulling something to make it look as if Andy's not guilty," he accused.

"I didn't say that," the sheriff protested.

"Well, I heard the saws, and we all knew that nobody was supposed to be cutting in our woods. Not right there, and certainly not on a Saturday. We both heard men yelling like they were mighty mad at being caught." Beau's face was getting hot.

"That did sound like what you meant, Tom," said Chris, laying his hand on the boy's shoulder. His voice was quite soft, but it held a deep note like a warning.

"You really do think he's innocent, don't you, Chris?" The sheriff sounded puzzled.

"I know Andy. I know enough about his affairs to know he doesn't need to do this kind of thing, even if he was the sort who would. And I haven't seen a scrap of evidence to change my way of thinking."

The sheriff's face, too, was getting a bit red. "I can't reveal my source, but it's reliable. You can depend on that. Andy Hartley is the only man in the county with that shade of red hair, too. You've got to admit that."

Beau interrupted with, "There's me. My hair's just like his."

"Man," the sheriff emphasized. "Someone with a red head just like Andy's was seen driving a truckload of logs off Temple land, out of a closed area. A truck that hadn't any right to be there. When the officials looked, they found they'd lost a good stand of pole timber. The best in the area, they'd been saving it for a rise in the market."

"So why didn't you arrest him right then?" Beau's voice was challenging.

"Not enough evidence. Nobody saw his face, and these two boys...."—he nodded at Beau and Arthur—"...swore they were in the woods with him all that same day. Looking for cinnamon bear, of all things!"

"We was, too! Looked for that old bear all day!" Arthur sounded indignant.

The sheriff sighed. "Now you know there's no bear left around here."

Chris winked at the boys secretly. He knew. He had seen her, too. "That's what folks say, sheriff," he said.

Beau poked Arthur before he could open his mouth again. It was their unbreakable rule not to talk about the endangered species, the few bears, the wolves, or the long-tailed cats. Cougar were hardly ever seen, any more, even in the deepest of the forest. Some fool had shot one only last year. There were too few wild things left in the woods and too many idiots who thought they had to shoot anything that moved, particularly if it was scarce. Lucky thing the big critters didn't range far from their protected areas.

The sheriff rambled on. "You've got to admit that you're prejudiced in Andy's favor, Chris. Going with Louise and all." He drove with much concentration now. Beau had gestured for a turn into the rough path the loggers' trucks had made. The path made the graveled road look like a super highway.

Chris grunted. "I knew Andy a long time before I met Louise. There are lots of folks likelier than the Hartleys. They're not dirt poor, don't need money all that badly. Andy pays his bills on time, keeps his balances up at the bank, but not so far up that it's suspicious. Farris Palmer's people have known Hartleys for generations, and that ought to tell you something. Bankers don't go out on limbs for other folks unless they know for sure and certain they're not going to be let down. Besides, I'd have thought you'd look twice at the Morfews. They're poor as pig tracks, for all that land. Old Turbo wouldn't know a law if he ate it."

Ralls shook his head. "They're not bright enough to sell the stuff this slick. Besides, I've got the older boy watching woods for me. He's a wonder at sliding through timber without being seen or heard. Set a thief to catch a thief, so to speak. There's nobody in my experience who won't steal, even your Hartleys."

"Your experience hasn't been right here. You must've been exposed to some bad ones, but these are peculiar folks, Tom. The crooked ones like the Morfews will steal your teeth while you're eating dinner. Everybody knows them and watches them like a hawk. The honest folks will starve before they'll get behind on a debt or take what's not theirs. There are some in-between, but Andy isn't one of them. He would not steal. Not anything for any reason." There was an edge of anger to Chris's voice. "If you'll look past the Morfews and the Rances and the Hardestys at somebody like Andy, then I don't know about your judgment."

The sheriff risked half an eye toward Chris. "Whoa! Whoa! I didn't mean to rile you up!"

They swung around a sweet gum, and the front wheels of the Plymouth dropped sharply into a chug hole. The sheriff muttered something that sounded dirty. Then he got out, followed by Chris and the boys, to look at the damage.

Beau saw at a glance that the road from here on in would be too rough for the low-slung car. "It's only about a half-mile from here, sheriff," he said impatiently. "Why don't we walk the rest of the way?"

"Guess we better," the big man growled. "Don't

want to bust up the county's property."

Beau and Arthur bounced ahead, leading the men to the clearing. Beau pointed out the faint trace where Andy had gone through the brush toward the spot where the cutting had been done. There wasn't any readable sign that any of them could see, though they all searched earnestly. Only the truck tracks in the soft sand, a few scuffed man-tracks, and those of the boys, where they had searched for their brother, could be found.

The sheriff hunkered onto the sand. "Look here, Chris. This is the same kind of tire track we've found before."

"You thought those were from Andy's trucks," Chris said shortly.

"Haven't seen anything to convince me these aren't. He could have met his friends and driven off with them."

"Leaving his little brothers to worry themselves to death?"

"He knew Beau and Arthur could find their way home."

Chris's mouth thinned to a line. "You're just being stubborn, Tom," he sounded cross. "All you've got is a mighty weak case, a mighty unlikely case, and you know it."

"It's the only one I've got," protested the sheriff.

"While you're looking up the tree where the possum isn't hiding, the critter itself if sliding off into the brush, laughing at you." Chris muttered.

Beau looked from one to the other, his eyes anxious.

"Will you look for Andy anyway?" he pleaded.

"No matter what you think, he's really gone." This wasn't going the way he had thought it would go. He never thought that the sheriff might not look at all.

Ralls looked down at him and seemed to notice for the first time the real terror in the boy's eyes. "Of course. Of course. Nothing would suit me better than to catch up to that crew, whoever they are. If Andy should be with them, I couldn't possibly arrest him for taking timber off his own land, now could I? I surely want to know who's with him."

Beau looked over at Chris. Chris shook his head, just the least bit. No more argument, right now, he signaled. Beau was so angry he was shaking, and he found it hard to keep his mouth shut.

They looked through the stand carefully, poking into every spot that looked promising. There was nothing in the dug hole that Beau had stumbled into, which relieved him more than he let on. There was nothing anywhere else, either, and after a while the sheriff drove them back to the house. He radioed in what little information he had before he left. Chris stayed there with the boys.

Before the dust from Ralls' wheels had settled, Beau sat down on the porch. His legs had suddenly given out on him, and he dropped heavily. He looked up at Chris.

"I always thought that the law was to help people when they were in trouble. I never thought.... Chris, what are we going to do?"

Chris reached down to put a firm hand beneath his chin, raising Beau's face until their eyes met. "Andy's smart. Remember that. He's no panty-waist, either. He's smart, and he's tough."

He looked off toward the west. "The chopper ought to be in by now. I got permission to take it out. You boys come along with me. Probably too late to see anything but we'll try all the likely routes, anyway."

Even with all his worry about Andy, Beau found his heart thumping with excitement. A ride in a helicopter didn't come along every day. He hurriedly scribbled a note for Ma and Louise, saying that he and Arthur were with Chris. He didn't mention Andy's disappearance. He felt that that was something better told face to face than in a note.

For both of the boys the ride was a first. Neither had been higher than the top of the biggest sweet gum in Ma's yard. Beau found that his knees were trembling, as he climbed in after Arthur and was strapped into the seat beside the open door. Arthur was wedged into center position, his eyes round as walnuts.

Chris was watching them, though he didn't seem to. Beau could feel a glance form the corner of his eye, and he had a feeling that Chris knew that he was frightened. Yet from the expression on the young man's face, Beau thought also that he was proud of both boys for hiding their fear so well. Then the engine revved up, and conversation was impossible in the din made by the chopper blades. Dust boiled up around them, then branches were at eye-level, and they were airborne.

The ride was terrifically exciting. The boys bounced and pointed and tried to talk, though any sound they made was drowned out in the whipping noise of the blades. Words weren't necessary, though. Their excitement filled the bubble.

"There!" cried Beau, after a while, pointing down at two trucks on a threadlike road below. Twin dust-storms followed the vehicles, as they moved along the graveled track. Chris dropped the chopper low enough to see the trucks well, hovering just ahead and to one side of them.

"No." Beau said, shaking his head. Neither was one of the trucks he had seen in the woods.

They kept at it, moving along the winding routes of county roads, graveled roads, even logging tracks, but there was nothing to see except an occasional pickup or car.

Late in the afternoon, Chris pointed to the fuel gauges. He shook his head. They'd have to go back now, the boys understood. The chopper rocked as he curved eastward, climbing rapidly.

Beau stared at the sunset. The scarlet sun slanted long rays across the dark cushion of pines in the forest below, touching the black-green with salmon light. A small lake slid beneath them, making Beau gasp and point downward. It was like golden metal, poured into an irregular mold, shining impossibly brightly in the strange light. Chris grinned and swung slowly to hover for a moment, until the light changed and the water was, once more, just dark water.

As they turned again eastward, Beau lost his exaltation. Beautiful? Yeah. But Andy was lost. What had happened to his brother?

CHAPTER EIGHT

Things happened too fast, leaving Beau no time to think about them, to sort things and figure out what to do. Andy was gone without a trace. That left Beau with no place to turn, he felt deeply. He needed desperately to go off by himself and get his thoughts into some kind of order.

Chris set them in their own front yard, amid a storm of dust and blown leaves from the chopper blades. As he lifted the craft into the sky again, he waved goodbye. Then he was gone over the surrounding trees. He had told them that he would do something. But what? What could Chris, or anyone, do until some new fact came to light?

Arthur was tired, hungry, and irritable. Beau left him in the kitchen, making another monster sandwich.

"You think you can tell Ma and Louise what happened?" he asked the younger boy from the doorway. "I've got to go off by myself for a while, before my brains blow the top of my head off."

Arthur nodded, his mouth full of the first bite of the sandwich. "Ooh-goor-hd," he said, through a mouthful of food. Beau took that to mean, "you go ahead," so he went.

He headed straight for his thinking tree. The tree had once been deep in a thicket of hardwood. Struggling for the light had made the mimosa spread its branches wide, seeking out every stray gleam that penetrated the heavy leaf-cover above it. Now it was an umbrella, a wide circle of branches that swept to the ground on every side. Something, lightning, maybe, had split the tree when it was young. That made it grow out of a Y-shaped crotch about three feet from the ground. Six feet above that, one side forked again, into three large limbs just right for sitting and leaning back.

Beau discovered the mimosa when he was very small. He remembered Pa telling him that it wasn't really native to the East Texas woods, but that the climate and the land were so well suited to it that the species had gone wild all over, competing where it could get a toehold among the native kinds of tree. He had always loved the tree, spending many hours of his time, before he was old enough for school, among its comfortable branches. The years hadn't made it any less attractive.

He still liked to slip away from the house, where Ma was famous for finding chores for him as long as he was within eyeshot. That was where he read books, wrote school papers, and plotted strategies on his small magnetic chessboard. And dreamed and watched and just enjoyed BEING.

Every year, he had fought a running battle to keep the mockingbird from building a nest in his tree. Otherwise, the feisty little bird would attack him, every time he began climbing into his favorite spot.

When Pa had logged out the big hardwood that

had surrounded the mimosa, it reveled in the sunlight it had fought for so long. The branches spread until on one side they made a canopy across the road that loggers used in taking hardwood to the mill. Later, that road came to be used by neighbors and friends as they went from the county road to the river, and Andy hadn't minded. He even kept the worst ruts graded and filled. A couple of times a year, he would take Beau and Arthur with him to put up barricades on both ends of the road. Posted signs went up, just for a few days. Otherwise, an old law of right-of-way would have made it public property. Most of the time, though, it was open to any comer.

"We'll give anybody the right to use the road," Andy said, "but we'll not give away one inch of our land to anybody."

Nobody but a woods-person could see the dimly defined track as it left the county road. Those who knew and used the way were woodsmen like the Hartleys. They used it to pull their boats down to the river, but they never trespassed on the Hartleys' land in doing that.

Yet, if one of those fishermen had looked closely as he drove almost beneath the old mimosa, he probably wouldn't have seen Beau sitting up in his nook, all but hidden by the lacy cover of leaves. He'd found a good hiding place.

This evening, Beau pulled himself up with more difficulty than usual. His legs were still stiff with effort. The last light was fading from the sky, and he was bone-tired, discouraged, frightened, and angry. The mimosa rustled to him, though the branches were almost bare, it was so early in the year.

He lay back against the center limb and gave himself up to the fascination of watching the sway of the branches, the tight curls of leaf-buds. A squirrel was barking in the woods. An early whip-poor-will was whimpering. A hoot owl protested, and cried out, deep in the forest toward the river. There was nothing like sitting and listening to smooth out the wrinkles in your mind, Beau thought.

When he heard voices above the sound of a slow-moving four-speed pickup or jeep, he wasn't surprised. Saturday night was a good time for fishermen to be going to the river to run trot-lines or do some night fishing. A twin swath of light swept across the trees, as the vehicle twisted and turned to follow the trail, and as it passed he could see by the reflections that Gaitor Morfew and his brother Taintor were in the jeep.

That surprised him. The Morfews had plenty of river frontage of their own, even after the lake property was taken from their place. They didn't need to come this way at all. As they seemed to resent fiercely that while they had lost land to the lake the Hartleys had lost almost none, he was astonished that they would come near Hartley land.

As far as anyone knew, all the Morfews did was fish and hunt for their living, though old Turbo had been known to put in a scanty corn crop from time to time. Privately folks said they ran a still and sold white lightning, which would account for the money they always seemed to have. That was probably what became of Turbo's corn crop, Beau thought. He sat very still and listened, as the jeep passed almost beneath him.

They were arguing. that was clear from the

tones of their voices, but the words were hard to understand because of the noise of the motor and the rattling of the jeep.

"When you hunt hogs, you're bound to pick up a few ticks!" Taintor yelled at his brother. That came clearly to Beau's ears.

"Maybe," Gaitor growled. "But I never figured on nothing like this."

Taintor said something that Beau couldn't catch, though the tone of his voice sent a chill down the boy's backbone. Only the end of the sentence came through clearly. "...All of them and that Ranger, too. I'd like to put all of 'em under the Devil's Jawbone!"

Beau shivered. The Devil's Jawbone was a red granite slab that thrust itself up through the trees of the Sabine National Forest, rising even higher than the surrounding wood. It was a fearsome thing, violent in some still, ominous way. The spooky thing was that it was unrelated to every other geological feature of the land around it. Not even the geologists had been able to explain how it came to be there.

A local saying had grown up about it. To be under the Devil's Jawbone meant to be dead. Though he had heard no names, Beau felt sure that the Morfews were talking about his family, as well as about Chris.

The jeep moved forward, out of hearing, and Beau slipped down from his perch in the tree. If the Morfews were on Hartley land, mean-talking about his folks, they must have been up to something that they shouldn't've been doing. Something near the river? Probably. There just might be something there that would tell him where Andy might be.

"There he is, Taintor!" It was Gaitor, who must've slipped back on foot. "I told you I seen somebody up that tree as we passed!"

Beau had thought that the dim light and the spreading branches would hide him from view as they passed below him. He had reckoned without Gaitor's woods-trained eyes.

Without waiting to see what they might want, he dug in his heels, sprang forward, and ran for all he was worth. He could hear brush crashing behind him, but he didn't look back, even when Taintor called, "Come back, boy. We want to talk to you."

He ran as he had never run before, even that morning when he had strained himself to what he thought had been his utmost. Not toward home, either. The Morfews had come around and put themselves between him and the house. He headed, as if by instinct, for the deepest woods, the only place he knew that might be a real hiding place.

The Bog.

He had never been closer than the hardwood forest outside its edges. He feared it with both the fear any woodsman feels for such unchancy things and that familiar fear that his own family had such reason to know. The Bog was more dangerous, particularly at night and for one unfamiliar with its few and hard-to-find trails. Beau knew that, come what might, he must escape from the Morfews.

The sounds of pursuit stopped. Beau halted, his breath searing in his lungs. A second shirt was now shredded by sawvines and haw bushes, and more scratches crisscrossed those he had received that morning.

Raw lines laced his ribs and stung as sweat from

his run touched them. He was trying so hard to keep from panting and still catch his breath that he almost missed the faint sounds of the other boys as they slipped toward him. The Morfews were as good in the woods as he was.

He held his breath, tried to slow his pounding heart. He dropped to the ground. In the dark, all polecats smell the same. He just might be able to slip out of this box and confuse his pursuers so they couldn't know who was chasing whom. If he could do that, he just might get away.

A quavering hoot with a trace of phoniness about it told him where Gaitor was. He slid along the ground toward the source of the sound. There was no light at all now. The thickness of the forest cut off any starlight there might have been. Only by moving his hands cautiously ahead of him could he avoid deadfall and other obstructions that might crackle and give away his position.

Now he was behind Gaitor, he thought. He could see a bulky shadow move against a lighter background. He drew in a breath and gave to perfection his most treasured imitation, the spine-chilling quaver of the screech-owl. Gaitor yelled and jumped clear off the ground, which gave Beau much satisfaction. There is nothing spookier than having a screech owl sound off at close quarters in the blind black woods at night.

"Taintor, he can't get away from here without your hearing him. I'm going back to the jeep for flashlights," Gaitor said, his voice a bit shaky.

"Right. If he moves, I'll nab him," came the answer.

Beau lay still against the ground, wondering if

Taintor had him spotted. In this darkness, it seemed unlikely. He could make out the shape of Gaitor moving away toward the jeep. Now seemed a good time to find out.

Moving his hands before him again, he began inching away from the spot from which Taintor's voice had come, but the older boy was good. The whole thing had been a ruse to make him move. Beau saw Taintor the instant before he reached down and grabbed a tatter of his shirt.

"Now I got you!" Taintor said.

Beau came straight up from the ground with a yell. He literally ran up the front of Taintor, carrying him off-balance backwards and knocking the breath from him. Once Beau's feet touched ground again, he was running. This time he didn't stop to listen for any pursuit. He knew it would be there. They were more experienced than he was, being older, but he knew these woods like his own front yard. They didn't. That would give him an edge, if he could find a way to use it. Being scared half to death was a help, too. His legs found new strength, and his breath was coming easily again. Good old adrenalin!

The Bog was almost five miles from the Hartley house. He had done something like a third of the distance in his first spurt before they trapped him. With shaking legs, Beau topped the slight rise that turned into a long slope and lost itself in the first dank reaches of the Bog. Beyond this point, the smelly waters covered almost everything. He always avoided the place, not only because Ma and Andy insisted on it, but because he had a horror of it.

He hesitated, feeling a touch of anger that Andy

93

hadn't seen to it that he learned the ways of the Bog. He taught him almost everything else. Still, he couldn't blame Andy too much. He still remembered too vividly the way Pa and those other people had driven accidentally into the Bog, down into the Sinky Hole, to disappear instantly beneath the murky waters. Even the jeep hadn't been found. The quicksand never gave up anything, except at its own infrequent times. There was good reason for the Hartleys to hate the Bog.

A branch cracked behind him, and Beau held his breath, letting it out slowly, silently. A whisper came to his ears.

"There!" They had him spotted again.

Everything depended on the Bog now. He was committed, like it or not. He had to go in and take the chance that he might never come out again. Pa wandered the Bog all his life. Andy did, though he didn't much like doing it. Could he?

He wondered briefly if the Morfews would dare to follow him. Then he drifted down the slope as silently as the mist moved in the dawn only that morning. He found time to marvel at that. Now tendrils of mist from the damp ground twined about his ankles. He shivered.

Gaitor yelled, "There he is! Quick, Taintor, he's going into the Bog! Don't let him get in there!"

They broke cover to come crashing through the growth toward him. That was the motivation he needed.

Beau turned from the solid land and waded as fast as he could manage into the dark waters of the Bog.

CHAPTER NINE

The black water and the black night melted together. Not a flicker or a ripple told Beau that he
had entered the water. Just the wash of blood-warm
fluid over his moccasins, turning them into slimy
hindrances, indicated that he was really in the fringe
of the Bog. He slipped off the sodden messes on his
feet and hung them on a low branch. Maybe he
could find them, given a chance to. Maybe they'd
dry out into something usable. Maybe he'd survive
this night. Maybe.

He kept on going, hoping that he wasn't circling, as people had a tendency to do when in the
woods. Still, he did have some clue: there was a
constant peep of tree frogs, crickets, and night birds
from behind him, where the solid woods grew.
Ahead were different sounds. An alligator's boom-
ing cry. Deep-throated "BA-RA-roomps" from big
old bullfrogs. If he kept his ears open, he thought
that the slight differences in night-sounds might
guide him.

On the other side of the Bog, just a few hundred
yards, lay the Andrews farm. Mr. Andrews had a
phone. If he could just make it through, there was
help, both from neighbors and at the end of the

phone line.

He needed to talk to Ma. By now she knew that Andy was gone, nobody knew where. By now she must suspect that Beau was almost certainly in trouble as well. She must be frantic with worry.

Beau stumbled over a cypress knee and fell flat. The fall probably saved his life. His hands, flung out before him, sank into oily sand. They felt as if something were sucking them downward, along with his face and upper shoulders. He was in quicksand!

Holding his breath, he thought frantically. What was it Andy had told him? Ah. Yes! He pushed down and back in a sort of inverted breast-stroke. He felt his face moving upward, through the muck. Slowly, slowly, he held himself flat on the top of the sinkhole, pulling himself back toward that last bit of solid ground where the root had tripped him. When he was on his feet again, he was trembling so hard he could barely stand.

He was afraid before. Now he neared panic. Turning back, as well as he could tell, he tried to retrace his steps. Even the Morfews looked to be better than the Bog at night, but the fall and the fright had turned him about. He didn't know which way might lead to the safety of the hardwood forest. There were no landmarks at all.

An alligator boomed off to his right, and Beau stopped in his tracks. Panic would kill him as surely as quicksand would. He knew that. Slow and easy, that was the only way to proceed.

He stood quite still, listening to the racket of the forest at night. The idea of woods being silent was a myth told by those who never went there. The dark was alive with noise. The frogs were growing louder, varying their songs from tinny bleats to bass-horn mooings. A fish, it sounded like a really big bass, struck at something in the deeper water off to his left. Jar flies chee-cheed their weird calls. A hunting owl hooted, and there came a soft, slithery sound at his feet that ceased with a quiet ripple of water. Probably a moccasin, and him standing there barefoot. He shuddered.

A whip-poor-will sent his whimpering cry through the wood; something crashed deep in the swamp. It was too noisy. All the sounds hid any rustle or footfall that his enemies might make. A step in any direction might well take him right into their arms. Beau stood, shaking, unsure what to do, or which way to run. The soft rasp of cloth against cloth sounded behind him. Beau jerked, tensed himself to run, but two strong hands grasped him. He felt his knees go weak, and his heart pounded away, fit to burst out through his ribs. All his instincts told him to run, to fight, but there was no strength left in him.

Then a familiar voice breathed into his ear, "Easy, Beau. Keep still and don't say a word."

The boy froze, a thousand questions echoing through his mind, but he said nothing, waiting for orders from Andy.

"Here. Catch hold of my belt."

"Andy, how did you get here?" the question burst out before he could stop it, though it was a whispered query.

"Not now," Andy hissed. "We may still have company."

Beau felt his brother move, and he set a hand on

either side of Andy's waist and let the motions of his body guide his own steps. In Indian file, they moved away, Beau setting his feet in Andy's tracks, as nearly as he could judge in the darkness. There was no sound to mark their going.

A pale sliver of new moon rose high enough to peep, now and then, through the thick canopy of leaves overhead. It didn't illuminate their way one bit. Instead, it made the rising wraiths of bog-mist look like a convention of ghosts trailing through the Bog. Beau had never seen anything so creepy in his life.

The water was sometimes hip deep. Once Andy said, "Careful, now," as they made an abrupt turn around a palmetto stump. With every step, Beau's cringing foot felt for reassurance, the squish-plod of solidity beneath its sole. Always, it was there.

An alligator coughed roughly, very near at hand. Andy paused for a long moment, his hand patting Beau's at his belt, before going on.

It seemed like hours, maybe even days and years, to Beau. The world shrunk to Andy's belt, the water about his knees or hips, the ratcheting noises of the swamp. Safety seemed to be something far away and faintly remembered. At last they moved upward, not much, but enough to set their feet on dry ground. Some invisible island that rose in the midst of the swamp? Beau waited to find out.

Andy said, "You can let go, now," and Beau's hands unclenched from the strip of leather that had meant the only security there was. In a moment, Andy had a fire going.

He saw they were in a small hollow surrounded by rocks, crowned with tremendous trees. The hollow's edges were littered with what looked like pet-rified bones and other strange shapes. A low wall of the stuff had been erected, and in the middle of the roofless room it formed, Andy kindled his fire.

Andy looked across the blaze at Beau. "Now you can ask away," he said, his white grin flashing in the firelight. Beau was by now too weary to ask anything. He sat abruptly, arms across knees, and bent his head down to rest.

Andy came over and looked down at his young brother. The state of the boy's clothing told him much. His own were in a similar condition. He bent and touched Beau's berry-bush hair. "Hungry?"

Beau nodded without lifting his head. Suddenly, he was famished. When had he eaten? Not since making that sandwich in the kitchen, this morning? His stomach gave a doleful growl.

Andy pulled a battered skillet from a niche in the rocks behind him. Beau sniffed, then his head came up and he looked into the vessel. Browned squirrel in its own juice! He reached out and took a back leg, stripping it of meat in two bites. His chewing was loud in the cup of the walled space.

Andy, busy with his own meal, didn't chide him. He knew starvation when he saw it.

Swallowing the last of his share of the squirrel, Beau wiped his lips on his tattered sleeve and looked at Andy. "We didn't know what happened to you," he said. "We looked and looked. Chris took the chopper, and we all looked from there for the trucks we had seen."

"I know." Andy set aside the bones in the skillet and leaned forward, arms about knees. "I've had a mighty busy day, and I hate it that I had to leave you to worry. But I found out who's stealing the timber. I even found out where they're taking it, where the last loads are right now, and where it's being sold."

The meat and the warmth were bringing Beau back to life. Questions welled up in him. "Where were you? We were scared silly when we heard all that arguing, and then you were just gone. The sheriff is looking, as well as Chris."

"Things moved too fast. Here, let me start tracking the possum at the henhouse. That way, we won't miss anything." He handed Beau an apple from his mysterious store and the boy settled back against the petrified-bone wall to listen. Andy's telling took a long time, but he knew that when they were done everything would have been said.

"You remember, we heard the saws," Andy began, but he didn't wait for any reply. "I left you and Arthur and slipped up to see what was going on. I crept up to the edge of their cut and hunkered down in a thicket to watch. They had two hauling trucks and a really old Ford with an A-frame. Taintor Morfew was using the A-frame to load, and Gaitor and four young guys I didn't know were doing the cutting."

"Young guys? How old?" interrupted Beau.

Andy shrugged. "About Taintor's age, roundabout. Why?"

"Gaitor is always bragging about his tough cousins from Houston. Might be, it's them."

Andy looked thoughtful, the firelight flickering on his face and bright hair. "Now that just could be. They looked a little like the Morfews, now I think about it. And they surely are just as mean. You saw how they cut?"

Beau nodded, and Andy went on, "They didn't cut any of the big pines, the ones that are really valuable. They just were taking little piddling saw-logs. They'd probably have taken pole logs, if there had been any there, but these old trees are just too big for that. Thing is, they weren't after the pine at all. They cut the old wolf walnut right off at the ground. Didn't leave an inch of the wood. In fact, they dug down and took a lot of the roots, too. They were filling in the stump hole and covering it up with dirt and pine needles when I slipped up on them. Chris told me that tree was worth a mint, all by itself."

Beau clenched his fist against his knee. "I think I stepped in that hole. Funny, I didn't miss that tree. I should have. Something looked strange, but I was so busy looking at the downed pine and trying to see tracks that I didn't even think about the walnut. It's all twisty. Why would it be so valuable?"

"Veneer, Beau. Those hardwoods have a grain pattern, especially in a twisted tree like that one, that makes them almost as valuable as gold. They slice it thin and overlay furniture with it. You can cover thousands and thousands of dollars worth of furniture with just one tree as big as that one.

"Anyway, they loaded the pine on one truck and were loading the walnut on the other. By the way, the cab on the truck hauling that load of pine was the same color as our truck's, and the driver was wearing a cap that was just about the color of my hair." Andy poked the fire with a short stick of wood.

"Taintor knows the woods. He's got all the instincts. He felt me watching them, and I was so intent on seeing what they were doing that I didn't notice when he slid off into the trees. He came up behind me. The first I knew of it was when he grabbed me and yelled for Gaitor to come and help him hold me.

"I tore into him and took some lumps before I could fight free. That is some big, tough character, let me tell you. But I caught him in the eye with a good lick, then I tore off into the woods as fast as I could go. I went away from you boys. I just didn't want them to know you'd been there. You never know what that kind will do, but they didn't follow me. They left me and started getting those trucks out. I cut through the trees to the county road and laid for them, hiding on the overhanging limb of that big old white oak that arches over the road."

Beau was bouncing up and down, now, his weariness forgotten. "Just like on TV!" he exclaimed.

"Yeah." Andy grinned, embarrassed. "Just like TV. I could have used a stunt man. He'd have been mighty handy, because when I dropped out of that oak into the leafy branches still left on that walnut I nearly killed myself. Never got so cut and bruised and winded in my life!"

He pulled up the tail of his shirt to show a deep gash along his ribs. Dark bruises covered his chest and back, and many smaller cuts and gouges gleamed redly in the light of the fire.

"I must have been knocked out, because I don't remember anything about being on the gravel road or the highway. When the truck left the main road and started hitting ruts, I came to, mainly because it hurt so bad." He tucked his shirt back in and poked the fire again.

"We were on a little old trail that never had been a road. After a while they slowed all the way down and we crossed the road that leads to the Devil's Jawbone Lookout. Then I knew where we were. They took that load right spang through the National Forest on tracks that I'll bet even Chris doesn't know are there. They went right down to the river. When it was in sight and I reckoned they were about to stop, I slid off the back of the tailgate and hid in the woods."

Beau listened with full attention. "I ran through to the county road, too, but it never dawned on me that you might have done the same thing. That's why we couldn't find a trace of you. What happened then?"

A long cry sounded, way off on the upland side of the swamp, and Andy's head went up, his face turned toward the sound. "Cougar? I hope so. Oh, I hope so!" he murmured. Then he looked back at Beau.

"Well, they've really got an operation going down there. There's a backwater cutoff that looks so thick and brushy that even the river fishermen don't go in, and that's where they slide the whole wooden frame off the back of the truck and ease it into the water. Then they lift the chains that hold all their brush together and float frame, trees, and all over to the Louisiana side. They've got a winch built into a cypress stump, over there, and they hook on the frame, haul it out of the water, and unload the prime wood onto another truck.

"That truck can either move off at once or wait for another load until it gets full. They had a big pile of dogwood there...stumps ten to twelve inches through."

"Dogwood?" Beau was astonished. "Why'd anyone cut a dogwood? They don't seem to be good for anything but flowers in the springtime."

"They are valuable, too, Beau. I read somewhere that the finest cloth is woven on looms that use dogwood shuttles. They bang those shuttles back and forth through the warp of the cloth so hard and fast that nothing but dogwood is tough enough to stand up under the treatment. It draws down a high price, because it's scarce and getting scarcer. Only a few really big trees are left, and the clearcutters are taking out everything that stands to plant pine seedlings, so not many more are growing. Most of the big ones are in protected woods like this. There's several thousand dollars, over there across the river, in cut logs that they've creamed off this side."

"That's what was wrong with that first cut I saw," said Beau. "There used to be a big patch of dogwoods there. Big trees, and a lot of young ones, too. That was another thing I missed because I was looking at the downed pine."

Andy nodded. "Right. The pine was just an afterthought, a red herring to throw us off the track of what they were really after."

"Why didn't they just truck out the timber from right there? I don't understand why they took all the trouble to pretend to cut pine, and then haul all the stuff across the river."

"Safer, for one thing. The water's deep for miles up and down that stretch of the river, especially in spring. They might even have floated some of the logs all the way down to wherever their buyer is camping. You know, people see pine being trucked up and down the highways all the time and they're used to it, but if you saw a big old walnut tree like that, or a load of dogwood traveling, you'd take notice, wouldn't you? That's got to be the reason they're floating it to their market.

"The buyer was at the river, waiting for them. Did I tell you that?"

Beau shook his head. "You saw him?"

"Just a glimpse, but I was near enough to hear him just fine. He sounded like somebody from Alabama, by the way. Or Georgia. Someplace in the Deep South. He paid the Morfews on the spot. When they told him I'd seen them taking out the walnut, he told them not to bring any more logs for several weeks. Sure made them mad, too, but he didn't pay any attention. Just unloaded that walnut off the frame and sent them back across the river on it. Hard-nosed cuss, he was. I could hear him, across the water, perfectly clearly. Ma wouldn't have like his language."

"He didn't take the pine, too?"

"I never saw the pine. That truck must've turned off another way, because by the time I came to, it was nowhere in sight. I haven't a clue where they took that. Anyway, I swam across the river, as soon as it was clear to, and took a look at the log-load he had there. There wasn't one log of pine. Not even prime pole pine. Nothing but hardwood. A few really nice old walnuts, lots of dogwood."

The keening cry came again from the upland, and Andy poked up the fire and laid another chunk of pine-knot in the coals, where it sputtered as the resin began to heat up and catch fire.

"I moved downriver until I came even with our land, and then I crossed again. By then it was dark, and I was so dead beat that I couldn't see making it all the way home. I came in here for the night. To Pa's old camp. Ma knows I can take care of myself, and you ought to know it, too."

Beau felt embarrassed. "I do, Andy, really. It's just that we heard the fight, and then you were gone. We thought they'd kidnapped you, taken you clean off." He paused and looked about the walled room. "I didn't know about this place."

"Ma does. She used to come here with Pa, now and again. I've been meaning to bring you, now that you're old enough to keep a tight lip about things."

"I've been old enough for that for a long time," Beau said. "So is Arthur, most of the time."

"I suppose you both are, at that. It's just that I have a bad feeling about the Bog, nowadays. Don't trust it, if you see what I mean."

"Exactly where is this place?" asked Beau, looking about him. The low walls held the heat from the fire, and his clothes were drying, though the March night was chill.

"We're just about in the middle of the Bog. On an island. There's maybe a half-acre here that stays above water in anything but flood-time. I'll show you in the morning, but not too much. We've got a mighty lot to do tomorrow."

Beau looked up. "Tomorrow's Sunday. Ma doesn't like us working on Sunday."

"Ma will know that the ox is in the ditch for sure, this time. I've got to get the sheriff and Chris and take them over to that camp, before the buyer has time to move out his log-piles. Ralls will have to

106

notify the Louisiana authorities to meet us over there. With any luck at all, we can catch him and his crew red-handed."

"Let's go now." Beau stood up on weary legs.

"Whoa! I couldn't walk home tonight if I had to. I'm just too tired to go five miles through thick woods in the pitch dark. They're not going to get all those logs loaded onto trucks before we can get there. There were too many. For tonight, the best thing for both of us is rest."

Beau sank back onto the ground gratefully. That sounded good to him. He had run for miles, twice over, today, been worried half out of his mind and scared the rest of the way. It was time to rest, but one thing bothered him.

"Andy, what if the Morfews come in here after us?"

Andy grinned, but he didn't look amused. "They'll have to take care of themselves. I'm too bushed to pull them out of the quicksand tonight."

He stepped out of the little enclosure, and Beau could hear him snapping off branches from nearby trees. In a few moments, a shower of pine straw and cypress needles almost buried the boy where he sat.

"Make your own bed," Andy laughed, as Beau sputtered, "and be quiet about it. I'm going to sleep."

He did just that. Beau was certain that Andy didn't even hear his soft, "Good night!" after he curled, back to the fire, into his sticky and fragrant bed of needles.

CHAPTER TEN

A redbird's morning song woke Beau. Pre-dawn, that shrouded hush in which only the birds yet stirred and sang and he lay still, savoring it. Mornings were almost his favorite times, and then the memories of yesterday came crowding into his mind. He rose on his elbow and looked over at his sleeping brother.

A dark bruise covered one side of Andy's face from temple to chin. Through it grew a stubble of fine red beard. There was a long scratch on the arm outside his jacket, too.

Andy, feeling himself being stared at, even through a fog of sleep, opened his eyes without stirring, just as a forest animal could do. He moved, tried to sit up, and groaned.

"All those bumps and bruises stiffened up in the night," he complained, but he sat and began stretching, like a big ginger cat. "You about ready to go? We'll hike out and call the sheriff from home."

Beau stretched a bit, himself. His own muscles felt stiff as boards and terribly sore. Home seemed an awfully long way from this remote place.

"Let's go on to Mr. Andrews'," he suggested. "It's a lot closer, and we can phone from there."

Andy shook his red mop. "No, Ma's had enough time for worrying. Let's get home as fast as we can."

For all his haste, Andy moved through the swamp with agonizing slowness and care. Even in the safety of the forest, he didn't hasten the pace. His own soreness, as well as Beau's, forbade much speed. As they crossed the Bog, Andy pointed out to Beau the landmarks that could guide his feet to the winding ridge of solid ground beneath the thick, dark water. "That stunted choke-cherry, there. You skirt it, close by, on the right. See? Muddy, but not sinky. The clump of button willow over there—that marks a deep pool. Always go well to the east of that. There's not too much that you can see here with the mist hanging. I'll bring you and Arthur in, one day, and show you exactly where to step, by daylight or by dark."

The ground-mist was lying heavy on the water, almost to a height even with Beau's chin. A layer of clear air was sandwiched between that and another layer of mist, and the trees appeared to have no tops, just black slices of trunk held between pale plates of fog. Only when you passed close by one of the trees could you see bark and branches and leaves. They seemed to grow out of the mist, become real and solid shapes, then to recede, flatten out like something in a horror film.

More than once Andy stopped to let a gator slide off a mud-bank into a pool or a muskrat splash into the water. Mostly, he stopped to let snakes get out of the way. Moccasins abounded, now that the weather had warmed. They saw king snakes, too, and blue racers, and once Andy stopped, stooped, and gestured for Beau to look closely. A coral snake looped its bright pattern of rings across the log before him, slithering into a hole where a branch had broken away.

Today they were after a different variety of snake. They had no time to stop and watch.

The underwater path Andy followed the night before seemed much shorter by daylight. Beau would have sworn that they had walked for miles, but it was only a few hundred yards. They slowed almost to a standstill, once they came near the spot where Beau entered the water. They listened intently, peered into the obscure deeps, but there was no sign of the Morfews. Apparently, they gave up and left in the night.

Andy knew every shortcut in the wood between that point and home. Even so, both were exhausted and ravenously hungry by the time they reached the house.

Ma met them at the door, looked at them sharply, hugged them so hard that it hurt their bruises, but she didn't say anything or ask a question until they were sitting at the kitchen table with steaming mugs of hot coffee before them. The coffee was strong, and that surprised Beau, for his had always been laced with milk. He looked at Louise.

"If you're old enough to roam the woods at night, you're old enough to drink your coffee black, like a grown man," she whispered.

Andy told his story from the beginning, between bites of scrambled eggs and hot biscuits, fresh from the wood stove. When he mentioned his cut, Ma made him stop eating to show it to her. She hustled off to get disinfectant and dressings, and Andy winced.

Beau thought a minute, then held out his foot, which had been gouged deeply during the long, barefoot trek homeward. Louise doctored that and brought out his school tennis shoes to wear until they could find or replace his soft moccasins.

Arthur was bursting with questions, once the tale was told from both sides. "Are you going back into the Bog?" he asked, his eyes huge in his thin face. The fearfulness of the place haunted his childhood, and he looked at Beau, who spent a whole night there, with something like awe.

Beau tried to look casual. "Oh, sure. Some time when we have this timber pirating thing straightened out."

Andy grinned, winking at Louise. Beau blushed. He knew he'd imitated Andy's superior tone that had been used on him for so much of his life.

Once the meal was finished and all the cuts and abrasions tended to, Andy phoned Sheriff Ralls. Beau listened with attention to the one-sided conversation.

"Yes, I can locate it on a map," he said in answer to Ralls' question. "And I feel sure that you should call the Louisiana authorities to meet us there...yes, Oh, yes. Definitely on their side of the river, well above the head of the lake." He listened for a moment, then he said, "I'll drive in right away," and hung up the phone.

He tried to call Chris, but found he had taken the copter out for morning patrol and wasn't due back in for at least an hour. "Will you have him call when he comes back?" he asked.

"Beau," he said, when he was through, "will you

stay close to home and talk to Chris when he calls? I've got to go in and guide the sheriff out to the log site. We need to get in there fast, before somebody takes fright and skedaddles."

Beau would have given his eye-teeth to go, too, but he knew that Chris needed to be filled in as soon as possible. "Okay. I'll stay. Give 'em a lick for me, Andy," he called, as Andy drove away with Louise in the Mustang. She insisted on this, feeling that Andy needed all the rest she could give him.

"Women." Beau grumbled, returning to the porch to swing his feet off the edge beside Arthur. "They do make a fuss about a little cut or bruise or being tired."

"Tell me about the bog," Arthur ignored Beau's complaint.

"Well, Andy must go in pretty often. He knows his way even in pitch dark, and he's got a little shelter built on the island where we spent the night. Has a skillet there, and some food, and goodness knows what else. We left before I could rummage around to see. He must've worked hard to build it up like that."

Ma's voice came from inside the door, startling him for a moment. "No, Son. That has been there for a long time. Even before your Pa used to go there. Some say it was where runaway slaves hid out, back before the Civil War. Your Pa used it as his thinking place. When he was worried or we'd had a spat, he'd go off and stay there until he'd got himself all smoothed down again. Violet! Honey, go chase the old red hen off her nest and into the woods. I don't want her setting again."

Violet skipped off happily to perform that noisy

chore, and Ma sat in the rocker gesturing for her sons to turn to face her. She looked closely into their faces then nodded as if satisfied with something.

"Your Pa was a woods man. That's all I've ever told you about him, because Andy and I agreed a long time ago that too much was said and guessed and tattled about already. We didn't see any use in worrying you children with it. He was a good man, never forget that. Kind to me and to you children, the most tender-hearted to animals that you'd ever see, but he had some funny ideas and peculiar beliefs and ways. For instance, he loved the woods just the way Andy does, and he thought that anyone who didn't love them just that way had something really serious and basic wrong with them. He thought some other things were so against nature that they couldn't be let to happen. He told me so, many a time about one thing and another.

"When he drove off into the Bog, there was a Mexican man and his daughter in the jeep, along with Pa and Elmer. Some say that Pa hated old Rodríguez and drove 'em all into the Sinky Hole deliberately. Maybe. He had that funny streak, like I said. Andy thinks it was purely an accident, but I never was sure.

"Be that as it may, they all went off into the Sinky Hole, and not one came out again. Not even the jeep showed a trace afterward. There was a terrible lot of fuss at the time, as you might imagine, but folks finally quit coming around and asking questions that neither Andy nor I knew the answer to. That's one reason Skipper went off to the Navy, I think, he just got sick and tired of being asked about it.

"You can see why we don't talk much about the Bog. Why we didn't encourage you young ones, as long as you were too young, to go there. Andy goes there more now than he did, for his own reasons. For me, I think it's best not to speak of such things."

Beau felt his heart thumping heavily in his chest. This was something that had clung like cobweb, invisible but tangible, about the edges of his childhood, but he never thought that Ma would come right out with it so plainly. He gulped.

"Didn't Pa say anything...before? Looks as if he'd have said something to somebody, if he was going to do something crazy like that," he said.

"Not one word. He hugged me, before he drove off, and he played with you boys like always. Then he went to take Elmer and his girl to town after their marriage license. Maybe what happened was truly accidental. I've always hoped so, anyway. But folks still talk about it, now and again, and you'll likely hear it told in many ways before you're grown up."

Arthur had said nothing, but now a long sigh heaved from him.

Beau nodded. "I've had a few people do some hinting around to me, but I didn't know what they were talking about. It didn't mean a thing to me. I wondered, though, what it was. Ma, does Andy go there often?"

"He's a grown man, Andy. I don't dictate his comings and goings, and he doesn't have to account to me. He's the man of this family, and he does as he pleases. He brings me flowers, or plants, sometimes. Things that don't grow anywhere else in the woods. So I know he does go."

"Will he teach me about the Bog now?" Beau

asked. Arthur's expression made him change that to, "Teach us, I mean."

"It's time, I think, that you both learned how to take care of yourselves there. The Bog exists. We own it. You're old enough to see and understand and keep still. There are things in the deep woods that belong only to the family."

The telephone shrilled, interrupting them. Beau jumped up and ran to answer it. The words that came barking at him over the line turned his face pale, and he hung up the phone and pounded out onto the porch, shouting to Arthur, running toward the jeep.

"Get the tractor, hitch up the disk, and turn a strip eight or ten feet wide all around the clearing of the yard!" he cried, vaulting into the driver's seat. "That was Chris. Someone's set a fire on the northwest line, and the wind may bring it this way."

He didn't wait, knowing that Arthur, woods-bred as he was himself, knew what had to be done and would do it as well as any man could. Fire was the most feared enemy the woods people had. In a few hours, a fire could eat up the profit of years of growth and careful management. Fire was unusual at this time of year, with the ground and the forest mulch still heavy with the rains of winter. Late summer and early fall, droughty months, were the common seasons, when dried grass was like tinder, and low humidity did nothing to damp the air. But this year it had been a dry winter and spring. The new growth was thin. Old dry leaves and winter-killed grass hadn't been sogged into humus, as would have been the case with a wet winter.

Now the pines were full of sap, and if the heat

built up inside them enough to explode them into flames, there would be the most frightful sort of fire—a crown fire.

Beau shivered as he drove. Chris said that he'd spotted the smoke as he turned back from patrol. He had made a sweep over the flames and saw someone in a jeep circling along the northwest line of the Hartley land, dragging a blazing bundle of canvas-wrapped branches. He had gone down to hover above the jeep, but it had driven into a thick over-hang of trees Still, he felt sure he'd recognized the Morfew boys. That surprised him. He didn't yet know what Andy had discovered. Beau wasn't sur-prised at all.

The boy smelled smoke long before he could see the fire...that clean, resiny smoke that rose from old forest with generations of pine needles and oak and hardwood leaves carpeting its floor. A heavy pall hung in the sky, as he snaked round the curves of the logging trails, taking those that angled in the direction he was heading.

Units from the Forest Service were already in place, when he jerked the jeep to a halt. Volunteers from town, as well as neighbors, were already on hand or straggling in. Mr. Andrews had come with his own tractor and was plowing a line around the leading edge of the crackling blaze. The Forest Ser-vice jeep, with its attached plow, was just disappear-ing into the woods, as Beau came up. He remem-bered other fires. When he and Andy walked the cooled woods, later, they hadn't understood how that jeep could go between the close places where the plowed track had turned the dirt...spans that seemed too narrow for Beau to spread out his elbows in, but he had no time to think of that now. A freshening morning breeze was driving the fire deeper into the Hartley woods.

Walker, the chief Ranger at the fire camp, which was already set up and functioning, had taken charge immediately as fire boss. When Beau asked what he could do, he was aimed toward a shovel. He grabbed it and pitched in at the point where he was told to. The morning went in an agony of scraping away grass and brush, widening the line they were trying to establish in front of the fire. Now and again a tongue of flame came sweeping toward him, and he dug dirt and flung it onto the blaze until it was vanquished. Sparks blew across the line, setting up swirls of smoke from tiny new blazes, and he dumped dirt on them, too. There seemed to be nothing left of him but eyes to see danger-spots, hands to wield the shovel, and legs to carry him forward.

It was past noon when someone too smoke-blackened to recognize caught his arm and took the shovel from his cramped hands.

"You take a break, boy. Go back and rest and get something to eat. I'll take this spot in the line," said a voice so raw with breathing smoke that he couldn't recognize that, either.

Though the air was as hot as any oven, the fire seemed quieter, the terrible crackling roar less frightening than it had been earlier. The air seemed hotter back at the fire camp than it had right on the line, and Beau wondered if that was because he had been so busy and so scared while he was up there. Chris was in camp, working with Mr. Walker in directing the heavy equipment still coming in. They were mapping fire breaks, in order to turn the blaze no matter which direction the wind turned. When Beau tapped him on the shoulder, he grunted absently that some two hundred acres had already gone up.

When there came a pause, Chris came over and sat beside Beau. "They grounded me." he grinned. "The chopper flies on a cushion of air, and a fire like this one eats up your cushion, if you go too close. So they put me back here where I could get a good look at the show."

Beau slumped on the folding stool he sat on. "I wish I didn't have to look, Chris. Andy's going to be sick when he sees this."

Chris sobered. "Don't I know it. Makes me sick, too. It's hard to believe that anyone could be so vicious and irresponsible."

Beau got up and headed for the food tent set up beside the main one and returned to sit beside Chris to eat the tray-full he'd collected.

"You don't know the half of it," he said. Between bites, he told Chris all the many things he and Andy had learned since the morning before. "It's the Morfews, anyway the two boys, for sure. Andy rode their truck right down to the river an watched them deliver their load on the other side."

"Hmmm. I suppose you didn't know, Beau, you or Andy either, that I spotted a still on their property a few months ago. Took the federal agents in after it. We didn't catch the boys there, but we tore up that still good and proper."

"So that's why they said they were going to get you, too," Beau finished the last bite on his tray.

"Well, they haven't got a one of us yet." Chris grinned at him again, then rose. "Enough of this lollygagging around. It's back to work for me."

Beau stood and stretched. The brief rest and the food gave him new strength, more energy. He was ready to go back and do battle with the flames again.

Walker stopped Chris, as the two left the tent. "The weather report says that we can expect a wind change any time. A west wind is going to push that fire right into the National Forest. Go down there and see how good a line they've put in front of the fired. See if we can shift some of the heavy equipment around to the east."

Chris nodded and raised his hand in a half-salute. "Will do," he said. "Come on, Beau. I'll walk down with you."

Walking toward that conflagration was spooky. Beau noted that Chris kept looking up into the tops of the big pines ahead of them, though they were well on the safe side of the fire line.

"What is it?" he asked, at last.

"You know what a crown fire is?"

Beau winced, then nodded. Every woods person knew about crown fires. Great heat could make the turpentine inside the big pines explode, turning the entire tree into a Roman candle, shooting out flames up and down and sideways with the intensity of a blowtorch—or even napalm. Anyone unlucky enough to be on the ground when the fire started running through the treetops, exploding everything it passed, had no chance of escape. Without speaking, they moved toward a cleared strip for the rest of their walk.

Someone shouted. Beau heard it and looked about for any danger, but by the time he saw the falling snag, it was too late to do anything. Burning fiercely, it toppled toward him. Time seemed to slow down, the snag to fall with terrible deliberation. His muscles were trying to move, to jump out of the way, but he, too, seemed caught like a fly in molasses. His backward leap was interrupted when his heel caught in a root. He fell on his back, stunned.

Chris, a step or two ahead of him, turned and saw what was happening. Instead of stepping out of danger, he threw up his hands and caught the blazing snag barehanded, throwing his weight against it to shove it aside and miss Beau by inches.

"You all right?" Chris asked. Beau could see that his teeth were clenched against the pain in his burned hands.

The boy got to his feet, suddenly light-headed. The close call had shaken him, and his breath had been knocked out, but he knew he was all right.

He also knew that Chris wasn't all right. Chris stood hunched a bit, his left hand gripping his right arm above the elbow. When Beau caught his wrist, Chris was shaking all over with the pain. Then Beau saw the hand, and it turned him sick.

"Golly, Chris, let's get you to the first aid tent!"

Chris didn't argue, and that told Beau how badly hurt he really was. The first aid people had few facilities, but they cleaned and bandaged the wound and gave Chris a shot of pain-killer.

"You better let someone take you to town," said the medic.

Chris shook his head. His color was returning. "Too much to do. I'll be all right." He went back with Beau to carry out the fire boss's instructions.

The fire was a long way from over.

CHAPTER ELEVEN

Turbo Morfew groaned, rolled over, and sat up. It had been a bad drunk—one of those that brought back things he didn't want to remember, but the faint tang of smoke in the air brought him around. A woodsman didn't live who didn't come alive at the smell of the forest burning.

The house was quiet. Only the thump of Pastor's tail against the floor of the back porch interrupted the silence. All the birds had stopped their talking because of the fire he now could sense with all his oldest instincts.

"Gaitor! Taintor!" he called. He squinted out the window at the sun, which looked big and coppery because of the pall of high smoke, Noon, at least. Those young 'uns ought to be somewhere around at this time of day. It ought to be Sunday, too, he thought. Yep, Sunday. No school. No work.

"You boys get yore tails in here!" he yelled again.

There was no answer.

The old man staggered over to the sink and dippered water from the well bucket. The chill sting brought him to himself, and he looked around for his pants. Once they were on, he struggled with his clod-hopper shoes and went onto the front porch. Taintor's battered pickup wasn't under the big tree.

"Now where've those kids got off to?" he wondered aloud. "Time I need 'em is just the time they pick to be out of pocket. Never was a woods fire that us Morfews didn't help to fight. No matter whose place, and this 'un looks to be over to them stiff-necked Hartleys. Theirs or the National Forest, or both." He pulled a ragged shirt off a nail in the front wall. No use to put on a good one to fight a fire in, he thought. Even a fire on Hartley land— Hartley! Lucky red-headed snobs, holding themselves higher that their neighbors whose land had been grabbed for the lake. They should've took a bit from everybody. That would've been nearer fair. The way it was, he'd lost his heart-woods, and the Hartleys hadn't given up anything but a thin edge of hardwoods. Just not fair.

The Hartleys weren't burning. Their woods were, and that was something different. A tree didn't pay no mind to the little old temporary man who claimed to own it. There it stood in the woods, growing fern around its roots and squirrels in its branches. Innocent.

Tears leaked from the corners of his eyes as he thought of his own slaughtered innocents, gone now beneath the lake waters, and that got him moving again. Shovel...they might not have enough. Bandanna to tie over his nose and mouth. Canteen—he regretfully dumped out the moonshine and filled it with water. Moonshine could get you blown sky high, in the middle of a fire.

Now, ready? Ready. He swayed down the rickety steps into the front yard. No pickup to drive...

them boys gone gallivanting in it. Just have to walk. He set off down the dusty track, grateful for the shade of the overhanging trees. Take a long time this way, no joke.

Then he heard the sound of the pickup banging toward him. Good! He'd take the boys back with him. Three Morfews was worth a dozen anybody elses in fighting a woods fire.

He waited in the middle of the road. The pickup heaved up in front of him, and Taintor's grimy face stuck out of the window.

"Pa! What you doing way out here, walkin'? You better go back to the house. You'll hurt yourself, the way you're weaving around."

He shook his head, his long greasy hair flopping into his eyes. "No. Got to go help fight that fire. See that smoke? Woods're burning, over toward the Hartleys. Scootch over, Gaitor. Taintor, you turn around and head that way. We're goin' to show them red-headed Hartleys what Morfew can do!?

Taintor grinned nervously. "Get on in, Pa. We'll take you home. We've already showed 'em, Gaitor and me. We really showed 'em what Morfews can do. We set 'em afire, Pa. They're going to lose a lot of timber, maybe even their house, if the wind stays right. What do you think of that? You've hated 'em ever since their land wasn't took and yours was."

Turbo stood still in the road. The waver went out of his stance. He seemed to straighten, to stiffen. Something inside him was crying out in pain, but he kept it in, didn't let even a moan escape. All those trees, burning, groaning, going up like torches....

He stared at his sons, and for the first time in weeks his eyes were clear and sober. He saw them.

124

He saw himself. Sickness rose in him, but he squelched that, too.

"You...set...the...woods...on...fire?" he asked, so slowly that they waited tensely for each new word.

The two boys couldn't answer. They only stared back at him, their eyes wide and panicked.

CHAPTER TWELVE

The day moved on to night. They worked without letup, feeling the flames always there, always waiting for the opportunity to leap the frail cuts and tear into the untouched woods. Men fell from exhaustion, from smoke-inhalation, from burns. Nobody just quit and walked off. Nobody ran away, though more than once the was reason to.

The west wind drove the fire ahead of it into the National Forest land before their fire lines could be established. The equipment had to be loaded onto trucks and brought around ahead of the fire to try catching it further on.

Now and again Beau glimpsed Chris on the line. For a while his bandaged arm showed up whitely against the smoke and grime. Then it was black, like everything else. He didn't have time to call out to him, though. Beau just kept on working, digging and scraping and throwing shovelfuls of sand onto sparks. He no longer could tell by feeling when his arms lifted the load. He couldn't tell if he was hitting what he threw the dirt at, either. He seemed set on automatic, working on and on without really knowing what he was doing.

He was startled when Walker came up behind

him and set a hand on his shoulder. "Okay, Beau, I think you've done enough. We just about have the line complete and the fire contained. You go back to camp. I need for you to do something for me," he said.

Beau tried to hand the shovel to the man who stepped into his place, but his fingers wouldn't let go. They seemed welded to the handle, and once the thing was loosed from his hand, he felt lost without it, as if it had grown to be a part of him. He staggered away toward the camp, so exhausted that he didn't even sit down until someone came up and guided him toward his jeep. The boy followed in a daze and let the man, so grimed with smoke that he didn't recognize him, help him into a seat beside the vehicle. A cup of warm sweet coffee appeared in Beau's hands, and he sipped at it, his head clearing a bit.

Then the man spoke, and Beau recognized the chief Ranger. Walker was the dirtiest human being Beau had ever seen. His hair was singed, his eyebrows and lashes gone. Holes had been burned in his clothing by flying sparks until he seemed to be wearing lace, and his hat was coal black. Beau would have laughed, but his face was too stiff with weariness to stretch that far.

"Think you can drive, Beau?" Walker asked.

The coffee revived him a bit. Feeling was returning to his body, enough to tell him how tired he really was and how many places ached or stung. He didn't want to do a thing but sit right here and sleep for a week.

"I think I can," he said. The fire wasn't over. His timber was safe, now, what was left in this area, but the National Forest wasn't. He had to help in any way he could.

"Good boy!" Walker sounded almost as tired as Beau felt. "I want you to take Chris to town. He's out on his feet, and that burn is really bad. He won't quit as long as he's here, but the doc says he'd better rest. The only way to get him to do that is to get him away from the fire."

Beau shook his head to clear it. "I don't want to drive on the highway, Mr. Walker. I don't have a license, and besides I'm too tired to know what I'm doing. It's not safe. Why don't I take him to our place?"

Walker nodded decisively. "Even better." He looked at Beau with the ghost of a twinkle in his red-rimmed eyes "He'll probably listen to Louise before he will any of us, anyway. I'll get him."

Beau climbed into the driver's seat of the jeep. It wasn't easy. He carefully set his left hand on the wheel and his right on the shift lever. That was easier than moving it back and forth. He was tempted to lean his head forward against the wheel, but he knew he'd be asleep instantly, so he kept it rigidly erect. He mustn't relax, even for a moment. Once he went to sleep, nothing on earth was going to wake him up again.

Mr. Walker came back leading a figure even more scarecrow-like than he was. Chris's shirt, torn and burned, flapped about him, one sleeve completely gone, the other lacy with spark-holes. The bandage was as gray-black as his skin. When the chief ranger led him to the jeep, Chris folded himself into the seat, but he was still muttering.

"...Need me, I feel as if you will. Can keep going. You just watch...."

"Don't either of you worry," Walker said. "The fire's pretty well contained, now. Fresh crews are coming out any minute. They're on their way. You've both had enough, for now. Go rest. There's going to be a lot of mopping up to do.

Chris subsided. Then he looked over at Beau with a puzzled expression. "Is that you, Beau?"

For the first time it occurred to the boy that he must be as fire-blackened and dirty as the others were. He managed to answer, "Yep."

Chris tried to grin, but he couldn't quite manage. He leaned back in the seat and closed his eyes. "Any time, Beau."

Walker patted him on the shoulder. "Take it easy, Beau, and be careful. Go slow."

Beau nodded. He was surprised to find that he had cranked the engine. He put the jeep in gear and crawled away along the rutted track. Smoke whirled at him out of the darkness; the road appeared and disappeared. The road home seemed the longest drive of his entire life. There were even times when he wondered if he weren't asleep and having a nightmare.

Chris made no sound, and Beau imagined that he must be trying to cushion the burned hand against the jolting of the jeep. Now and again the boy looked over at him, and even in the dim light from the dash his face was lined with pain.

Beau hoped that Louise would hear the jeep and be there waiting when he pulled up at the house, and she was, as he knew she would be. Her ears could pick out the sounds of any of the Hartley vehicles a half-mile away. She stood on the porch with Arthur, and they both ran to the jeep when it stopped.

"Oh, Chris!" Louise put her arms around the Ranger. He gasped, choking back a cry of pain, when his burned hand touched her. She turned loose at once and looked closely.

"Your hand!" she breathed. "Oh, Chris, I'm sorry!"

"It's all right, Honey. I'm all right," Chris managed to say, through gritted teeth.

Beau looked at his hands, clamped around the wheel as if they would never turn loose. He started making individual efforts to unclench his fingers, as Arthur stared at him, wide-eyed.

"I've never seen anybody that dirty before," the younger boy said, as the porch light revealed Beau's state. Then he glanced at Beau's hands, now moving slowly to release their grip on the wheel. "You're bleeding!"

Beau looked down at his hands as if from a great distance. He remembered the minor annoyance of blisters forming across his palms, earlier in the day. He even remembered when one set of blisters broke and began to sting from the sweat running into them. After that the fire had been too real and close, the labor of fighting it too great. There was so much excitement and fear that neither pain nor weariness was able to get a grip on him. He hadn't known when the blisters turned to raw flesh and loose skin. There was so much soot blackening his skin that the blood hadn't shown up at all.

Ma appeared beside him, though he hadn't realized that she was on the porch beside Louise and Arthur. Her hand touched his shoulder, pulling him from the jeep.

"Come into the house, Beau. Let's get you cleaned up so we can see how badly you're hurt. You look terrible, but I've seen men come from the fires looking a sight worse."

Beau would rather have closed his eyes and slept just where he sat, but arguing was more trouble than going along with Ma. Chris came, too, but he seemed to be moving terribly slowly, almost as if he were drunk.

"Doc gave me somethin' to put on the burns. In my pocket." The words were slurred with exhaustion.

Louise rescued the tube of antibiotic salve and helped Chris toward the porch. Once there, she removed what was left of his shirt, while Arthur undid Beau's buttons. The two stepped unprotestingly out of their pants and shoes and trudged away to the boys' bathroom in their underclothes, shepherded by Arthur.

The bath was between the room that Beau and Arthur shared and that in which Andy reigned alone. There was a comfortable walk-in shower, no tub, which made it easier. Beau didn't think he could've stepped into a tub to save his life. Chris went first, and Beau leaned against the wall, waiting.

The water was running, but he couldn't hear Chris moving around. With much effort, the boy pulled back an edge of the curtain and looked in. Chris had dropped the soap from his wounded hands to the tile bottom of the shower. The Ranger was just standing there looking at it. He looked as if he were about to slide right down on the floor under the cool sluice of water and go to sleep.

Beau caught him just as he was about to slip,

leaning his full weight against Chris to hold him against the side of the shower stall. He yelled for Arthur, who bounced in, took one look, and said, "Uh-oh!"

Between the two of them, they got most of the grime and soot off Chris and led him out of the shower. Arthur draped a towel around his middle and led him into Andy's bedroom. They aimed him at the bed, and he fell onto it, out already. Arthur tucked a sheet and a light blanket over him, once he was stretched out, and Beau felt certain that Chris never knew when they left the bathroom.

Arthur learned fast. He took Beau back to the shower and shoved him into the stall. "You stand still. I'll wash you off. Lean against the wall, if you need to."

Beau remembered the first gush of cool water. He remembered leaning; he never recalled the bath or being led to his own bed and tucked in. His very last memory was of the bar of soap escaping from Arthur's grip and being chased over the slippery tile, a hundred miles away or so, down by his feet.

He slept with a smile on his face.

CHAPTER THIRTEEN

There was nothing but fire. Gaitor Morfew was driving a red jeep through dry grass, followed by a roar of flame.

Beau looked up, and the pines were shivering, their needles pulled this way and that by the convection currents caused by the heat of the blaze. Suddenly they were terribly still. Beau felt rooted, immobile. He could hear Chris's voice....

"She's going to crown!"

Still he couldn't pull his feet out of the earth that held them. Andy was outside the fire someplace, calling something to him, but he couldn't understand.

The red jeep zoomed toward him. Straight at him. He tried to run, to leap aside, but he was petrified. The bumper came nearer and nearer. Beau shrieked and sat up in bed.

Louise came into the room and sat on the edge of the bed. "It's okay, Beau. You just had a nightmare, and that's perfectly understandable after the day you had. You lie back now. Are you hungry?"

She was smoothing his hair, the way she did when he was little, and that brought him around to see where he was and to understand that he was safe. The mention of hunger finished rousing him.

He wasn't hungry. He was starved. "Oh, am I hungry!" He moaned. "My stomach's welded to my backbone."

"Thought so." She smiled. "If I ever see you when you're not, I'll just call the undertaker. It'll be too late for the doctor."

As she went off toward the kitchen, Violet crawled onto the bed and leaned one sharp little elbow on Beau's ribcage. "Sissy says you're hungry enough to eat a live polecat."

Beau chuckled. "Almost, little Stinky. If you don't get your elbow out of my ribs, I just might start on a live sister!"

Violet giggled; then she lay down and snuggled close without touching his ribs. "Do you hurt? Chris hurts real bad!"

Beau felt his heart give a big thump. "How is Chris?" he asked. How could he have forgotten to ask about him, first off, nightmare or no nightmare?

"He woke up, after you and Arthur put him to bed. He was moaning and moving around. Dr. Jim came and stuck some needles in him, and then he went back to sleep. I don't like having needles stuck in me, do you?"

"Not much," Beau admitted, "but sometimes they're better than being sick."

"That's good, because he stuck some in you, too. You were already asleep and didn't know it."

Beau tried to think back, but there was no memory of Dr. Jim or of needles. "Ma says that what you don't know can't hurt you." He sighed.

"That depends entirely upon the situation," said Louise from the doorway. "Move over, Violet."

She sat on the bed again, balancing a round tray on her knees. Steam rose from a bowl of creamy-gold soup. A large glass of buttermilk with floats of yellow butter sweated beside it.

"No steak," Beau grumbled, his eyes twinkling.

"Open your mouth. Take what you can get and don't grouch."

She filled the spoon and held it out to him.

He tried to curl his fingers around the spoon-handle. His fingers wouldn't cooperate.

"Here," Louise said. "I'll feed you. Open up."

Like some oversized baby mockingbird, Beau opened his mouth and took in a spoonful of cheese-flavored chicken soup. The bits of chicken were diced fine enough to be swallowed without chewing, as were the carrots and potatoes that floated in the rich liquid.

Beau swallowed. "Tell me about Chris," he said before he opened for another bite.

Louise lost her smile, though her hand steadily spooned soup into him. "Oh, Beau, he hurts so much. That arm is badly burned. He only slept for a little while, after his bath. Then he woke up and lay there shaking and groaning until we called Dr. Jim. He came right out here and gave him a shot for the pain. Dr. Jim seemed awfully worried. I think he's afraid that Chris might lose that arm."

Beau stopped eating. A moan came from deep inside him. "He got hurt saving me!" he said. "Louise, Chris was burned holding a burning snag off me until I could get out of the way."

She nodded. "I know about it. Mr. Walker came by while you were sleeping. He told us all about the fires, and he told Dr. Jim to do whatever was best for Chris, to get the very best, whatever it cost. They decided to leave him here with us. The hospital is full of smoke-inhalation cases from the fire."

She set aside the tray. "By the way, it's Tuesday morning. You slept all the way through Monday."

"I'm missing school."

"I am, too," she said, "but I think we can both be excused, just this once."

"In that case," said Beau, "I think I'm going back to sleep. My eyes won't stay open."

She patted him, pushing the bright hair away from his forehead. "I'm not surprised. Dr. Jim said to let you sleep as long as you could." She smiled down at him. "Sleep well, Brother."

Beau noticed that he wasn't "Little Brother," any more.

"Wake me up if Dr. Jim comes again and I'm still asleep," he mumbled.

"I promise." Louise smiled, herding Violet ahead of her out of the room. "Come on, Little Sister. Let's let Beau get some rest."

He lay back with his eyes closed, but the sleep he craved wouldn't come. After a bit, he got up and pulled on a pair of clean jeans. He went to Andy's door, across the hall, and peeped in.

Ma saw him and nodded for him to come in. She was sitting in the rocking chair beside the bed, watching over Chris.

Chris was so flat. Only his toes and the big white mound of bandages around the burned arm seemed to make any lump at all beneath the sheet. Chris's brush of dark hair made the only color in the bed. His tanned skin had gone pale, and he was terribly still.

136

"Ma, he looks awful," Beau whispered. "Why doesn't Dr. Jim bring an ambulance and take him to the hospital?"

"The fire filled up our little hospital, Beau, didn't Louise tell you? Dr. Jim said we could give Chris better care right here, where there's not a bunch of hurt people needing attention all at the same time. He's going to call a friend of his who is an expert on burns to come take a look at him."

"It was just a burn, Ma. He didn't seem to be hurt that bad, and he went back and fought the fire, afterward."

"When he should've quit and had help with that burn. That 'just a burn' almost burned his arm off. He probably was in shock when he went back to work, and nobody there seemed able to make him quit. There's infection in it now, and fever. Our friend is a mighty sick man."

Beau shivered. He sat down close to her feet, as he used to do when he was small. "What'll I do, Ma? It's my fault he got burned!"

"Did you start the fire, Beau?"

"No...but...."

"Did you make the snag fall just when you were standing under it?" she kept on.

"Of course not."

"Then blaming yourself is fool's talk. You were doing what you should have been doing, and Chris did what he should have done. He'd do the same again tomorrow, just the same way, to help somebody. He's that kind of man. You'd do it, too, if you had the chance. Now wouldn't you?"

She sounded so stern that it hardly seemed like Ma who was talking to him. But then she cupped her hand behind his head and pulled him forward so she could put a kiss on his forehead. He leaned his head against her knees for a moment.

When he straightened, he said, "I guess I'll go back and sleep, now. If there's anything I can do, you call me."

"I will, Son," she promised.

At the door Beau paused and turned. Ma was smoothing Chris's hair back, as she had just smoothed his. He felt better. Ma's hand held something much more than just touch. Beau thought maybe it was love. She always made him feel better, no matter what was wrong with him, and he felt sure Chris could feel it, even in his sleep.

When Beau waked again it was to the ringing of the phone. Nobody answered, though it rang and rang, and a chill of fear touched him. he slid out of bed and ran across the hall.

Chris grinned at him from the bed. Not much of a grin, just a faint shadow of his usual smile, but it was aware and alert.

Louise sat beside him, holding onto his good hand while Dr. Jim and a stranger in an Air Force uniform fastened a plastic bag full of creamy liquid onto the burned arm.

"This ought to be done in a hospital, Jim, where we can watch and control it," the stranger was saying to Dr. Jim. "Can I move him tomorrow?"

"Where to?" Chris's voice was a hoarse whisper.

"Would you believe the Air Force hospital at San Antonio? My plane is at the Beaumont Airport. I'd like to take you back with me. We've had remarkable results with this treatment, but always under controlled conditions."

"Anything you say," Chris replied. "But so soon?"

"Why not?"

Chris glanced at Beau, than at Louise. "I guess I want to be in on the end of this thing. I want to see the pirates and the arsonists caught. I've got a stake in this, too, you know."

Louise squeezed his good hand. "Andy has a way of working things out, Chris. You just do what the doctor says. We'll be sure to keep you right up to date on what happens."

"You should go," Dr. Jim said. "Major Tucker knows his business, and we don't want you to lose the use of that hand."

Arthur, kept from school on an emergency basis, was almost pushing himself into the space between the doctors and the bed, he was trying so hard to hear what was being said and to see what was being done. At last Major Tucker looked down at him.

"Want me to fix you up with one of these, Boy?"

Arthur stepped back very quickly. "No, sir. No, thank you. What's that stuff in there?"

"A whole lot of things." The Major winked at Dr. Jim. "Mostly antibiotics and pain killers."

Chris whistled softly. "They certainly are pain killers. Look. I can even move my fingers a little."

He did it, too, before the doctors were able to stop him.

"Don't get too frisky," the Major said. "The idea of this is freedom to move, so the scar tissue is less. Let's give it time to start healing before we take up finger isometrics."

The phone began ringing again, and this time Beau caught it on the second ring.

"Howdy." Andy's familiar voice brought a hundred questions immediately to mind, but Beau wasn't given time to ask them.

"I'm in Beaconsfield, Georgia, Beau. Along with Sheriff Ralls and some state police from Louisiana, Texas, and Georgia. We've got everything just about wrapped up over here. We wrung a lot of information out of that Alabama man down on the river, and we found the very mill where the pirated stuff was being taken. I'll tell you all about it when I get home. Tell me about the fire, how much was burned?"

"We lost about three hundred acres. Somewhere around five hundred in the Sabine Forest went, before they controlled it," Beau told him, along with everything else he knew so far. "I just woke up, so I haven't heard the final tally. But Chris got hurt. Bad."

Andy's anxious questions got the whole story out of Beau in quick time, and Beau kept assuring him that Chris would be all right. Then Ma took the receiver from Beau and told Andy to hurry home. "That way you won't have to blow money on long distance calls," she said. "Money doesn't grow on trees, you know."

Beau, at her side, didn't have to hear Andy's reply. "Ours does." All the Hartleys knew that.

When they went back into the bedroom, the doctors were getting ready to leave. Chris was sitting up, his good arm around Louise. He was smiling at her with that special look that made Beau feel lonesome and left out. He almost felt resentment that

Chris was going to take Louise away from them.

Arthur must have felt a bit of what he was feeling, for he poked Beau in the ribs. "If they get married, will Chris be our brother, too?"

Beau stopped short. He hadn't thought about that. Andy was their guide to the woods, their teacher about the things here in the world they knew. Chris was from the outside. If he became their brother, he could be their guide to that other world, out there. Beau thought of all the things the big, gentle Ranger had done for his family. How kind he was, and how brave. The sort of brave that didn't make a big show, just was there when you needed it. How wonderful to have Chris for a brother.

"Of course he will, you dumb knot-head," he replied, turning to look over Arthur's head in his old superior way. He suddenly realized that that wasn't so easy, any more. Arthur was growing. In more ways than one. He showed a lot of courage, too, these past days.

Beau punched him lightly on the arm. Arthur looked up at him. They both grinned.

"Did Andy say if they'd caught the Morfews and those others at this end of the pirating ring?" Chris was asking.

An unfamiliar voice from the door startled them all. "No, they ain't rounded 'em up. They won't need to."

Everyone turned to stare at the speaker. Turbo Morfew stood just inside the door. "Beg pardon, Mrs. Hartley. I found out what they done. All of it, the thieving, chasing after your boy so they run him into the Bog, setting the fire. They've done even more, and I got it all out of 'em...." His voice trailed off, sad and shamed.

"How much of this did you know before today, Mr. Morfew?" Chris asked, his voice quiet.

"Reckon I knowed a good bit, Ranger. I knowed about the still in the woods, and about the pirating right along. But you know us Morfews and the woods. We was brung up in these woods. It's hard to think we can't do what we please in 'em any more. Likely it's my own fault that these boys got no respect for the law. I always had meat to eat or to sell, no matter what the season. Never got a license to hunt or to fish." He looked at Chris defiantly. "I tolerated breaking the law, but I got no use at all for any hound that'd set the woods on fire. I brung 'em in myself."

Chris looked sad. Beau could see that he ached for the old man, the old woods man who hadn't been able to change with the times. His sons had taken his clinging to the old ways to mean that laws meant nothing, instead of that in the old man's day there had been no laws. Now they would all have to pay for that inability to change and for that basic misunderstanding.

The old man stood in the doorway, ragged, dirty, but somehow proud. "I'm taking my sons to jail, Mrs. Hartley. Reckon I'll go in right alongside 'em. We'll wait for the sheriff."

Before she could answer, he turned and went out, pushing each boy ahead of him with a hand on the shoulder. The look that they gave their father told the onlookers that their father's shame and pain had already begun their punishment, but they had crimes to pay for. The sound of the Morfew pickup driving away had a sad tone to it.

"Well!" Chris's voice broke the spell that had clung in the room. "I guess if I'm going to San Antonio tomorrow, I'd better get some rest. Looks as if I got in on the end of things, after all."

"No more timber pirates," whooped Arthur.

"No more," agreed Ma. "My prayers are answered. Thank the Good Lord that's over."

Beau grinned, but he said nothing. Over? Not by a long shot.

When Andy got home there was going to be a lot of clearing-up to do. Probably trials to testify at. All sorts of things. He was going to make Andy take him to the buyer's camp on the river, and to the Bog. Right in. Andy would have to teach him, and Arthur, all about it, how to find their way to the island, and everything.

When he got back to school, Wow! The whole affair would have to be told and retold. It wasn't done with. The timber pirates were finished, maybe. That part might be over.

Now other doors were opening, and they were just the beginning.

About Ardath Mayhar

The author of sixty-two books, more than forty of them published commercially, **ARDATH MAYHAR** began her career in the early eighties with science fiction novels from Doubleday and TSR. Atheneum published several of her young adult and children's novels. Changing focus, she wrote westerns (as **Frank Cannon**) and mountain man novels (as **John Killdeer**). Four prehistoric Indian books under her own name came out from Berkley. Historical western *High Mountain Winter* was published by Berkley Books under the byline **Frances Hurst**.

Recently she has been working with on-line publishers. *A Road of Stars* was her first original novel to appear in print-on-demand format. Many of her out-of-print titles are now available from e-publishers fictionwise.com and renebooks.com; other novels are being published via the Borgo Press imprint of Wildside Press and Amazon.com.

Now in her seventies, Mayhar was widowed in 1999, after forty-one years of marriage, and has four grown sons. The bookshop she ran with her husband for fifteen years was closed after his death. She now works at home, writing short fiction and nonfiction, and doing book doctoring professionally. Her web pages can be found at:

w2.netdot.com/ardathm/

and

http://ofearna.us/books/mayhar.html

BORGO PRESS BOOKS BY MARYLOIS DUNN

The Absolutely Perfect Horse (with Ardath Mayhar)
The Man in the Box
Timber Pirates: A Novel of East Texas (with Ardath
   Mayhar)

www.ingramcontent.com/pod-product-compliance
Lightning Source LLC
Chambersburg PA
CBHW031129210626
46816CB00015B/1243